"I'm not asking for pity, Hannah."

"Good thing I wasn't offering any." Unable to resist, Hannah reached up and gently touched the scarred side of Tripp's face.

He covered her hand with his and turned to face her. In that moment, something flickered in his eyes and his gaze almost became tender. Hannah's chest tightened.

Then he released her hand and stepped away, his gaze returning to the mare.

"Mothers are supposed to protect their children," Hannah said, her voice shaky.

"Doesn't always work like that." He nodded toward the brick houses in the distance, home to the children of Big Heart Ranch. "That's what this place is all about."

Tripp faced her again and leaned close. His gaze skimmed her face as though searching for something. Then he stuffed his hands into his pockets.

"It's getting late," he murmured. "Good night, Hannah."

"Good night, Tripp."

The cowboy walked away, leaving Hannah trying to figure out what had just happened. They'd passed some sort of milestone in their relationship, but she didn't know if she should be pleased or terrified.

Tina Radcliffe has been dreaming and scribbling for years. Originally from Western New York, she left home for a tour of duty with the Army Security Agency stationed in Augsburg, Germany, and ended up in Tulsa, Oklahoma. Her past careers include certified oncology RN and library cataloger. She recently moved from Denver, Colorado, to the Phoenix, Arizona, area, where she writes heartwarming and fun inspirational romance.

Books by Tina Radcliffe

Love Inspired

Big Heart Ranch

Claiming Her Cowboy
Falling for the Cowgirl
Christmas with the Cowboy
Her Last Chance Cowboy

The Rancher's Reunion
Oklahoma Reunion
Mending the Doctor's Heart
Stranded with the Rancher
Safe in the Fireman's Arms
Rocky Mountain Reunion
Rocky Mountain Cowboy

Visit the Author Profile page at Harlequin.com for more titles.

Her Last Chance Cowboy

Tina Radcliffe

Recycling programs for this product may not exist in your area.

 LOVE INSPIRED BOOKS

ISBN-13: 978-1-335-47904-4

Her Last Chance Cowboy

Casting all your care upon him;
for he careth for you.
—*1 Peter* 5:7

This final book in the Big Heart Ranch series is dedicated to the staff and children of Big Oak Ranch. Big Oak Ranch is a Christian home located in Alabama for children needing a chance. Find out more about them at www.bigoak.org.

Thank you to Tim at ARCpoint Labs for taking time to answer my numerous questions on DNA testing. All errors are my own.

A great deal of appreciation goes to my wonderful agent, Jessica Alvarez, for partnering with me on this series. Thank you, as well, to my editor, Dina Davis, who helped ensure that this last book of the Big Heart Ranch series was as heartfelt as the first.

Chapter One

Trouble.

Tripp Walker sensed it the moment he drove around the bend. He hit the brakes as he came upon the beat-up silver Honda parked awkwardly on the shoulder of the two-lane road that led to Big Heart Ranch. Dangerous place to park, which no doubt meant the vehicle was disabled.

His gaze shot toward the sky to assess the weather. Several hours ago, a tornado watch had been issued for Osage County, Oklahoma. Conditions were ripe for dangerous storms and even a tornado. By the time Tripp finished his business in Pawhuska and passed through the small town of Timber, the watch had changed to a warning, meaning a tornado had been sighted.

Overhead, the angry gray clouds tinged with green crowded closer, making the threat of the first tornado of May all the more real.

When a ping hit the windshield and frozen pellets began to descend, Tripp made a split-second decision. Despite his need to get back to the ranch and out of the dangerous weather, he couldn't ignore the disabled

Honda. He parked a safe distance from the vehicle and flipped on his pickup's emergency flashers.

Pulling up the collar of his denim jacket, Tripp reached for his cowboy hat before he got out. He inhaled. The air smelled like a storm was imminent. *The smell of the ugly*, some folks called it. Rain and ozone mixed together.

Hail continued to fall fast enough to form shallow puddles of white as he headed to the Honda and rapped his knuckles on the driver's-side window.

The tinted window inched down a fraction and a woman's big brown eyes met his gaze. She stared for a moment, no doubt taken aback by the scar that ran down the left side of his face, stopping right beneath his eye. After eighteen years, he was used to people staring.

"Ma'am, do you need assistance? Is everything okay?" he asked.

"Okay? Not lately," she replied with a sigh.

"What's wrong with your car?"

"Apparently, I ran out of gas."

His glance swept the Honda, from the cracked windshield on the passenger side to the temporary tags hanging in the rear window. Colorado. Well, that explained the funny way the woman talked. Definitely not an Okie. But it didn't explain why she was driving around in this weather. "Didn't you hear the news of the tornado warning on your radio?"

"The radio is dead and my cell is off to save battery life." The window inched down a little more and her gaze followed his to the dark sky. "Has a tornado been sighted?" she asked.

"Funnel cloud south of here." Tripp frowned and turned back to the woman, whose face registered alarm.

"Why aren't there any sirens?" she asked.

"Too far off the beaten track. The only thing up this road is Big Heart Ranch."

"That's where we're going."

He barely had time to register the word *we* when a little girl, about five or six years old, poked her head into the front seat. She pushed back a riot of orange curls and grinned up at him. "We want to go to the ranch and see horses, Mr. Cowboy."

Tripp bit back a smile, his good humor fading fast as he realized the child was in the path of a tornado. "I'll take you to Big Heart Ranch."

"And who are you?" the woman asked, her gaze assessing.

"Tripp Walker. I'm the equine manager at Big Heart," he said, annoyance mounting. "Ma'am, we need to hurry."

The driver's-side door opened and a petite dark-haired woman stepped out. She opened the back seat passenger door. "I'm Hannah Vincent. This is my daughter, Clementine." The child sat in a booster seat and stared up at him while clutching a pink stuffed horse. She was dressed in clean pink jeans and a pink patterned long-sleeved shirt. Clearly, the kid had a penchant for that color.

"Come on, baby, we're going to the ranch." Hannah unbuckled the straps and pulled her daughter into her arms.

"Horses?" the little girl asked.

"Shh," Hannah said. "We can discuss that later."

Tripp glanced at Hannah's left hand. No ring. Though his head tried to stop him, his gut moved quickly to judgment. *Plain irresponsible.* Who ran out of gas in the middle of a tornado?

Irritation continued to brew as he ran a hand over

the scar on his face and worked to control the emotions he'd so carefully learned to stuff years ago. He'd spent a lifetime paying for the sins of an irresponsible single mother. Now the memories all came rushing back.

Hannah faced him with Clementine in her arms. "Is everything okay?" she asked.

"Just dandy." Tripp turned and headed to the truck. He held the passenger door open. Hannah lifted Clementine into the cab and then put her foot on the truck's running board. When she reached for something to hang on to, he took her arm and guided her into the truck.

"Thank you," Hannah said.

He offered a curt nod.

She pulled Clementine onto her lap and inched nearer to her side of the vehicle as he went around to the driver's side.

Once he got in, Tripp gripped the steering wheel and turned his head a fraction to meet Hannah's dark eyes.

With that tumble of wavy chocolate-brown hair that touched her shoulders, and a face devoid of makeup, she seemed harmless. But he knew only too well how deceiving looks could be. As if sensing his annoyance, Hannah moved even closer to the door.

They headed down the ranch drive toward a split-log archway with the words Big Heart Ranch burned into a hanging sign. He stopped the truck in front of a drop-arm barrier that kept unauthorized visitors out and put his key card in the reader slot.

"Is this the ranch?" Clementine asked as the arm lifted.

"It is," he said.

The child's orange corkscrew curls bounced when she turned to look out each of the pickup's windows. "Where are the horses?"

"They're in the barn because of the storm. You'll get to see them before you leave."

"Oh, thank you, Mr. Cowboy." She rewarded him with a huge grin. The kid had a smile that could warm even the most frozen hearts.

When his cell phone rang, Tripp pressed a button on the dashboard. "Walker."

"Looks like the funnel cloud jumped past us. Storm moving in. A big one," the mature female voice on the speakerphone said.

"Thanks, Rue. I'm bringing guests to the admin building."

"Guests?"

"A Hannah Vincent. She ran out of gas on her way to see the Maxwells."

The sound of papers shuffling could be heard. "The receptionist is out until Monday, but I'm looking at the appointment list she left and I don't see a Hannah Vincent. Is she here to see all of them?"

Tripp turned to Hannah, and she nodded.

"That's right, Rue."

"Well, no worries. I'll find them and we can sort it out." She chuckled. "Just get out of that weather."

"Yes, ma'am." Once again, Tripp looked at his passenger. "You have an appointment at Big Heart Ranch, right?"

"Not exactly," Hannah said.

"Not exactly?" Tripp exhaled and held back a biting retort. Though the tension in the cab was palpable, he focused on driving, staring straight ahead out the window where fat drops of rain began to splash on the glass as he approached the administration building.

His job was to manage the horses. It would be good

to remember that. Hannah Vincent was Lucy Maxwell's problem now.

Tripp pulled the truck into a parking lot and led them out of the rain and into the brick building. "This way." He opened the door to a small conference room where Rue Butterfield sat with a cup of coffee watching the news. The gray-haired physician and retired army general turned to offer their guests a welcoming smile. "Welcome to Big Heart Ranch."

"I hope I'm not…" Hannah began. She pushed back rain-dampened hair from her face.

"You're not." Rue stood. "Big Heart Ranch aims to be a refuge in the storm. Literally." She chuckled and held out a hand in greeting. "I'm Dr. Rue Butterfield."

"Hannah Vincent. This is Clementine."

"Clementine!" Rue grinned. "Now isn't that a unique name?"

"It's 'cause of my hair," the little girl said. "It's orange."

Tripp bit back a smile when Clementine shook her head back and forth, causing the bright curls to move with the motion.

"Your hair is quite lovely and I am certainly pleased to meet you, Miss Clementine." Rue offered a hand in greeting. "I'm Miss Rue."

"Rue. That's a nice name, too." Clementine shook Rue's hand and smiled, obviously delighted by the grown-up gesture. "Mr. Cowboy is going to show me horses."

Rue lifted her gaze to Tripp. "Oh, are you, Mr. Cowboy?"

He knelt down next to the little girl. "You can call me Mr. Tripp."

"Mr. Tripp." She scrunched up her face and looked hard at him. "You are a cowboy, right?"

"Yes, ma'am."

"Do cowboys keep their promises?" Clementine asked.

"Always." He stood and turned his attention to the television screen on the wall. "What's going on with the storm?" he asked Rue.

"Funnel touched down on Route 66. No damage reported. Looks like we're safe. For now, only thunderstorms."

"I like rain," Clementine said.

"So do I." Rue smiled at the little girl and then turned to Hannah. "You're here to see the Maxwells?"

"Yes."

"Did they know you were coming?"

"Um, no." Hannah adjusted the purse on her shoulder and clasped her hands together. "This was sort of spontaneous. I drove straight from Denver."

"That's a long drive," Rue returned.

"Yes. Thirteen hours."

"We paid our respects," Clementine interjected.

Rue's eyes rounded, reflecting confusion and surprise at the comment. "How did you say you know the Maxwells?"

"I'm a relative."

Rue blinked. "I wasn't aware that they had any living relatives."

"Neither was I… I mean, until recently," Hannah stammered, her attention on Clementine.

"So how is it you're related to the Maxwells, dear?"

Tripp kept his eyes on Hannah Vincent. She took a deep breath and looked up. Her gaze moved from Rue to him.

"If you don't mind, I thought I'd discuss it with the Maxwells," Hannah continued.

"Of course. I don't mean to pry."

Hannah offered a hesitant and awkward nod.

Rue glanced at Tripp and he returned her searching expression with a slight shake of his head. If she wanted answers, she was looking in the wrong direction. He didn't have a clue and he didn't want to know, either.

"How about a cup of coffee?" Rue asked Hannah. She picked up her own mug from the table and smiled. "Fresh pot."

"May I please have a glass of water?" Hannah asked.

"Certainly. We've got chocolate muffins in the break room. Our Emma is quite the baker." She cocked her head toward Clementine. "Would that be okay for...?"

"Yes. Thank you very much," Hannah returned.

"Come help me, Tripp," Rue said.

He narrowed his eyes at the good doctor, but she ignored him and started down the hall. When they entered the kitchenette, Tripp released a breath. "I smell a scam."

"Oh, don't be so cynical." She paused. "Colorado is where their parents died, and where the kids went into foster care."

"Okay, so why didn't she call and schedule an appointment? Why surprise them on a Friday afternoon?" he asked.

"I have no idea."

"I've known the Maxwells for eight years. I was their first employee. If they had family, I would have heard about it by now." Tripp began to pace back and forth across the tiled floor as he continued to mull the situation.

Rue shrugged and reached for two glasses from the cupboard. "They'll be here shortly, and I guess we'll find out."

Find out? He didn't want to find out. This entire situation made him uneasy. Tripp pulled off his cowboy hat and ran a hand through his short hair. All he wanted to do was go back to the stables and be left alone.

He froze at the sound of the big glass door of the admin building opening and then closing with a whoosh and a dull thud. Boots echoed on the tile floor, along with soft murmuring. The Maxwells had arrived.

It was like the still before a tornado, and after thirty-four years in Oklahoma, he knew better than to stand in the path of a storm minutes before everything was getting ready to break loose.

Hannah swallowed hard as she faced the Maxwell siblings seated across the conference table from her.

Lucy, Travis and Emma in person. All dark-haired with dark eyes and generous mouths accustomed to smiling. And they were smiling now, which was a good sign. The Maxwells were accompanied by their spouses.

Jack Harris, Lucy's husband, was an attorney. Emma Maxwell Norman's husband, Zach, a former navy SEAL, sat next to his wife. The man looked like he could break her in two with his pinky.

Travis sat holding hands with his wife, AJ, a pretty blonde in a denim jacket who'd entered the room with a straw cowboy hat on her head. She was clearly very pregnant.

Though Rue was entertaining Clementine in another room, they'd asked Tripp Walker to stay. The man was just like family, Lucy Maxwell Harris, the oldest, had said. Pretty scary family, in her opinion. He wasn't smiling and hadn't since she'd met him, except when he was speaking to Clementine.

The man baffled her. He'd been nothing but a gentleman when he had rescued them. And when she'd struggled to climb into the cab of his truck, the cowboy had held her arm and easily helped her. His touch was surprisingly gentle for such a big and disapproving man.

Right now, the cowboy's cool blue eyes were nearly ice as they pinned her. Hannah tugged her sweater close against the chill in the room and looked away.

A tiny niggle of excitement churned inside of her. Excitement even Tripp Walker's less than warm welcome couldn't dispel.

She'd started over many times in the last seven years, but this was different. For once, she wasn't hiding or running away from something. No, for the first time in her life she was slipping from the shadows into the light and searching for her future.

And maybe she had found it.

This could very well be her family sitting around the table. Except they all sat on one side while she sat on the other.

She silently prayed for help and grasped for a scripture to cling to. Her grandmother may have been misguided in many ways, but when Hannah was growing up she'd made certain they both were in the pew every Sunday.

Casting all your care upon Him; for He careth for you.

Yes. That would work.

Lucy cleared her throat and smiled. "I have to admit we're all shocked to find out we have a relative. Travis, Emma and I went into foster care after our parents died because we were told we had no family." She pushed her short dark cap of hair back and folded her hands on the table.

"Are you related to our mom's cousin? She's the one who adopted us," Emma, the youngest Maxwell, asked.

"I believe I'm related to your father. Jake Maxwell."

Travis grinned and leaned forward in his chair. "You're related to Dad? Really? How?"

Hannah hesitated, then met his gaze. "I think Jake Maxwell was my father."

Travis's grin faded away at the same instant that Lucy's jaw sagged. She turned to Emma, whose eyes were round with shock.

The silence in the room was even louder than Hannah expected. She let her gaze slide to Tripp. Stormy blue eyes met hers before he looked away.

Hannah held her hands tightly in her lap and willed her heart to slow down. She tried to relax her clenched jaw. In the last ten minutes, she'd destroyed years of orthodontic alignment.

"Do you have proof? A birth certificate maybe?" Lucy asked.

"My birth certificate says my mother is Anne Bryant and the name of my father is noted as *declined*."

The siblings looked at each other. Hannah could practically read their minds. They were doing the math. But she had already done that in Colorado and knew only too well that she was a year younger than Emma.

"I'm confused," Lucy said.

"Believe me, I am, as well," Hannah said. "I was born twenty-nine years ago last month. My mother died when I was too young to ask who *declined* was, and my grandmother wouldn't discuss my father." Hannah took a deep breath. "Clementine and I were in Denver for my grandmother's funeral. Until the reading of the will, I thought she was my only living relative."

"We're so sorry for your loss," Lucy said gently. "We

know what it's like to lose everything. But what led you to think…" She gestured with a hand.

"I inherited a chest of my mother's things after she passed." Hannah paused for a calming breath. Again, she reminded herself that she hadn't done anything wrong. "There was a Bible with photos of my mother and Jake Maxwell tucked inside."

"Surely there's more than one Jake Maxwell in all the world," Lucy said.

"I compared the photos to the Denver Public Library microfiche files with your father's obituary photo. That's also what led me to Big Heart Ranch."

Lucy grimaced and nodded.

"Could we see the photos you have?" Travis asked.

"Yes. Of course. They're in the trunk of my car."

The eldest Maxwell's gaze moved out the window to the pasture of tall grass in the distance. Then she slowly turned back to face Hannah. "I want to be sensitive to you, but this still doesn't prove that he's your father."

Hannah stared down at her tightly clasped hands for moments, recalling the letters she'd read over and over again.

Dearest Anne, you are on my mind constantly…

She raised her head to face the Maxwells. "There are also dated letters from Jake to Anne that indicate a very close relationship."

Lucy's face paled as she released a soft, anguished sigh and covered her mouth with a hand.

"I'm sorry," Hannah murmured.

"There's nothing for you to be sorry about," Travis said. "This has to be as difficult for you as it is for all of us."

"We could do a DNA test. Couldn't we?" Emma asked while looking at Jack Harris for a response.

The attorney reached out to hold Lucy's hand. "Sure, but as I recall, without paternal or maternal DNA, the results won't be absolutely conclusive, though they will show if you're family."

"I think we should talk to a lab and find out how to proceed," Emma returned.

"This is a lot to take in, Em," Lucy said. "That Dad had a relationship outside of his marriage."

"Four years before they died," Travis murmured.

Emma turned to her siblings. "We can't begin to presume to interpret the past. I don't think we should even try. I say we deal with facts. Hannah is here and for her peace of mind and ours we should find out if we are indeed family." She offered Hannah a sad smile.

Travis, too, offered a sympathetic nod. "All of our lives are affected if it's true."

Lucy met Hannah's gaze. "I have to be clear. The ranch is a charity. The land was given to us by our mother's cousin. The woman who adopted us. Big Heart Ranch is a sanctuary for orphaned, abused and neglected children. This ranch is our life mission, but we have no inheritance. Nothing."

Hannah's gut clenched at the words. Inheritance? If only they knew she'd already walked away from one. What she longed for was to find her place in this world.

"I'm here for the same answers you want," Hannah murmured. "Period."

Once again, an uncomfortable silence filled the room.

"Where are you staying?" Lucy asked.

"I saw a motel on the way in."

"The Rooster Motel?" A horrified look crossed Lucy's face. "Oh, you don't want to stay there. We have a nice bed-and-breakfast in Timber."

"That's not really in our budget, but thank you," Hannah said without looking at any of them.

"Well then, I'd like to invite you to stay at Big Heart Ranch, at the very least until we can figure all of this out," Lucy said while she looked to her siblings for confirmation.

Hannah held her head high. "I don't do charity."

"Of course not. We can always use help on the ranch," Emma said.

"What about Clementine?" Hannah asked.

"There is a licensed daycare at the ranch now," Lucy said. "How old is she?"

"Clementine is five. Almost six."

"It's May. Isn't she enrolled in school?" Emma asked.

"We've moved around a lot," Hannah said. There was no point sharing further details. Her past had nothing to do with the Maxwells other than when it intersected with theirs.

Emma frowned. "I handle childcare at the ranch and I can tell you that kindergarten is mandatory in Oklahoma."

"It's not in Texas, Kansas and Missouri."

"You certainly have traveled," Emma murmured.

Traveled. Hannah nearly laughed out loud. Not quite. She had been running from her grandmother's reach for nearly seven years. Staying one step ahead of the wealthy woman who insinuated that she could take Clementine away from Hannah if she so desired.

"I'm sure we have some area you could contribute to on Big Heart Ranch."

"What's your background?" Lucy asked.

"Recently, I've been a bookkeeper, cashier and mostly a cook."

"All useful skills." Travis shook his head. "Can you ride?"

"Yes, absolutely. I have an extensive background with horses. I've been riding since I was a kid. I worked in children's camps and equine clinics when I was a teenager and in college." Hannah paused and swallowed. "However, there's something you should know."

"What's that?" he asked.

"I'm pregnant." Hannah sat straight and proudly. Yes, she was a single mother whose husband had left her not once, but twice. But she refused to give in to the whispers of shame fueled by her grandmother that had dogged her for the past seven years.

"Congratulations," Travis said. He grinned like a preening peacock as he put his arm around his wife. "AJ and I have a baby due in August." He glanced over at Emma. "And Emma and Zach are expecting a baby in December."

"That's wonderful," Hannah said.

Emma chimed in, "When is your baby due?"

"Late December."

"Congratulations," Emma added, her face lighting up with genuine pleasure. "Oh, my, we're due at the same time."

"I'll add my congratulations, too," Lucy said. "As you can see, we love babies around here. Your…um, partner is with you in Oklahoma?"

"I'm recently divorced." She cleared her throat and once again focused on her hands, running her thumb over a ragged hangnail. Recently divorced because once he'd found out she wasn't going to be a wealthy woman, he'd walked away.

An awkward silence stretched before Lucy cleared her throat.

"You do understand what we do here at the ranch, right?" Lucy asked.

"Not exactly," Hannah admitted.

"We create a new normal for the children who come to live with us at Big Heart Ranch. We have two ranches here, the boys' ranch and the girls' ranch. The children are placed in a real house with house parents, not a dormitory. Though they aren't a biological family, they are a family of the heart. A forever family. Our children have daily devotionals, lessons, homework and chores, just like any other child."

Lucy looked to Travis. "We have been promising Tripp an admin to do the paperwork, scheduling and ordering supplies for about two years now, haven't we?"

Travis nodded with enthusiasm. He turned to Tripp, but the equine manager's face remained stony. The blue eyes flickered and his jaw twitched, though he didn't utter a word.

"We'd still have to run a background and fingerprint check," Emma chimed in. "It's ranch policy."

"Would you consider staying?" Lucy asked.

"I don't know…" Hannah murmured with a glance at Tripp Walker.

"Tripp?" Emma nudged the silent cowboy.

"If the Maxwells welcome you, then so do I." The words were a slow drawl, his gaze cautious, revealing nothing to indicate he'd changed his opinion about her.

Hannah was silent. So what if the horse manager didn't like her? This wasn't about her. She wouldn't knee-jerk and make a decision based on pride. Clementine and her unborn child deserved to be around family, if that's what the Maxwells really were.

"Thank you. I'll stay…for now."

She glanced around the table for a moment. Did she

dare to hope that Big Heart Ranch might be the end of the road? A place where she and her children would be welcomed unconditionally? Or would she always be searching for home?

It's in Your hands now, Lord, she silently prayed.

Chapter Two

Disoriented, Hannah sat up in bed. Something was off. Normally, she woke to the spring scents of hyacinths, daffodils and lilac that floated into her furnished apartment from the florist shop downstairs.

Her searching gaze landed on Clementine, who slept soundlessly in the next bed, cuddled into a softly faded multicolored quilt with her pink stuffed horse clutched to her chest.

Hannah blinked against the dappled sunlight sneaking into the room through the blinds and realized she was in a guest bunkhouse at Big Heart Ranch. Today was Saturday. She yawned as Friday's events came back to her.

"This is it," Rue Butterfield had announced when they arrived at the bunkhouse yesterday afternoon.

Hannah had enough money for one night at the Rooster before they'd have to head back to Missouri. Staying at Big Heart Ranch was an answer to prayer.

"This is where we're staying?" Hannah had asked Rue. The bunkhouse was a rustic log cabin cottage with six bunks, a small living room and a kitchen area. It was several paychecks nicer than her place above the floral shop in Dripping Falls. Yet, her grandmother would have been appalled.

"Yes," Rue had answered. "This is the guest bunkhouse."

Hannah had glanced across the room at a neatly made-up bed. "Who else lives here?"

"That would be me. I stay when I'm needed and, with summer coming up, that will be most of the time." She paused. "Oh, and Dutch will bring up your car and your bags. He put gas in your Honda."

"Dutch?"

"Dutch Stevens. Senior wrangler. Can't miss him. He's bowlegged and has a silver handlebar mustache."

"Please tell him thank you. And thank you. For all this." She had waved a hand around the room.

"You're family, dear." Rue smiled.

At that moment, something like shame had clawed at Hannah. *Family.* As far as she could tell, she might be the illegitimate daughter of Jake Maxwell. Family or not, she'd certainly put a pause and a huge question mark into everyone at Big Heart Ranch's thoughts yesterday.

Hannah glanced at the clock. It read 7:00 a.m. She wiped the sleep from her eyes and looked over at the two battered suitcases that the wrangler had brought to the cabin yesterday. Nearly everything she owned had been shoved into those bags or into a cardboard box in the trunk of her car when she'd left Missouri for her grandmother's funeral in Colorado.

She stared at the ceiling and considered the wisdom of leaving her job as a short-order cook at the all-night diner. The pay was regular and Clementine slept in the manager's office during her shift, saving Hannah a fortune in childcare expenses.

It wasn't the career she'd planned on, but there was no point in looking back. She'd learned long ago that the only thing certain in life was that she had to live with her choices. Big Heart Ranch it was. For now.

Just as Hannah swung her legs over the side of the bed, the strong waft of bacon, eggs and fried potatoes hit her full force. With one hand on her stomach and the other covering her mouth, she quietly headed to the restroom.

Morning sickness. She splashed cold water on her face and stood over the sink taking slow breaths, willing her stomach to calm down.

"What am I doing here, Lord? I hope this was Your nudge and not another mess up for You to get me out of."

Patting her face dry with a towel, Hannah brushed her teeth before coming out to the main area again.

"Morning, Momma." Clementine sat on the edge of her bunk, biting her lower lip as she concentrated on buttoning up her blouse.

"Well, look at you. No nagging you to get out of bed today."

Clementine raised her head and smiled, brown eyes sparkling. "Miss Rue said to get ready. Mr. Tripp is coming by to take me to see the horses after breakfast."

Hannah eased down next to her daughter on the bed and pulled a hairbrush from her purse. "Let me fix your hair."

"I have a twisty." Clementine held up a nylon hair tie.

"Good, because the snarls have taken over. I'll brush it thoroughly tonight," Hannah said as she pulled the springy orange curls into a ponytail.

"Thank you, Momma."

Rue popped her head around the corner. "Breakfast is ready. I made eggs, bacon and my special home fries."

"Toast would be good." Hannah swallowed, praying she wouldn't retch. "But you don't have to cook for us."

"I was making breakfast anyhow."

"Coffee?" Rue asked once Hannah had changed into jeans and a T-shirt and was seated at the table nibbling toast.

"Water is fine. I'll get it." She stood and moved to the sink. The coffee smelled wonderful, and she'd kill for a mugful, but that would wait until she could get decaf.

"What a good eater," Rue said to Clementine as she sat down at the table and picked up her coffee.

"She's filling her reserve tank," Hannah said.

The five-year-old scooped up another forkful of eggs and shoveled it into her mouth like a starving trucker.

"Whoa, Clemmie. Slow down there, good buddy," Hannah said.

"This is really good, Momma," Clementine said.

"Please don't talk with your mouth full." She put the water on the table and slid into the chair next to her daughter.

"Yes, Momma," Clementine said over a mouthful of eggs.

Hannah looked across the table at Rue Butterfield. The woman's serene smile said that all was well with the world. It was as if Hannah and Clementine belonged in this kitchen, at this moment. There was a peace in the room that Hannah hadn't experienced in a long time.

"This was very nice of you, Rue. I'm not accustomed to someone cooking for me."

"Mind if I ask how far along you are, dear?"

Hannah froze. "How did you know?"

"The morning sickness, and you turned positively green when you laid eyes on the bacon." Rue smiled. "I'd have never noticed otherwise."

"I'm eight weeks." Hannah placed a hand to her stomach. "I can barely zip up my jeans."

"You're slim as can be."

A knock at the door interrupted the conversation and had all heads turning. "Come on in," Rue called.

Tripp opened the door and removed his hat. The lean cowboy stood in the threshold surrounded by the morning sunlight. The man had to be at least six foot five. An inch or so more and he'd hit his head on that low doorway. He ducked as he entered the kitchen. The man had a thick head full of toffee-colored hair, trimmed short and neat.

When Tripp turned a bit more, Hannah noted that with his stubbled shadow and strong jawline, he was almost perfectly handsome. The scar running down his face only added to his rugged and dangerous appeal.

Appeal in general, she corrected herself. Not appealing to her. Nope. Things only became complicated when there was a man in her life.

She placed a protective hand on her abdomen when Tripp's frosty blue eyes assessed Hannah with an expression she couldn't define. It seemed the man was constantly sizing her up and each time she fell short.

"Coffee, Tripp?" Rue asked.

He held up a hand. "I'm good, thanks."

"Horses. Horses. Horses," Clementine chanted. She jumped up from her chair.

"Hold it right there," Hannah said. "Clear your place setting and thank Miss Rue for breakfast."

"Thank you, Miss Rue." Clementine put her silverware on her plate, turned to the sink and stopped. "I can't reach the sink."

Before Hannah could even get out of her seat, Tripp had gently lifted the little girl to the stainless steel sink.

"Thank you." Clementine giggled.

Tripp turned to Hannah as he lowered her daughter to the floor. "Ready to go?"

"Yes. Let me get our sweaters."

"Does she have any other shoes besides sneakers?" Tripp asked.

"Oh, I didn't even think… Clemmie, go put on your cowboy boots."

Clementine nodded and raced from the room, happy to return wearing her scuffed Western boots. The pint-sized show-off did a little jig of a dance ending with a small, "Ta-da!"

"You're a real cowgirl, aren't you?" Tripp said with a wide grin.

Hannah nearly fell over at the smile that lifted the corners of the cranky cowboy's mouth. It was a genuine smile that transformed the stone-etched face into swoon-worthy. For a fleeting moment, Hannah longed to make Tripp Walker smile again.

Then she remembered that believing in white knights who came with happy endings was how she'd gotten derailed in the first place.

Hannah followed Tripp and Clementine out the door. She couldn't keep up with his long strides, but her daughter skipped and jumped across the yard to the stables, splashing in a few mud puddles on the way, with joy shining on her face.

Tripp stood at the entrance of the big building, allowing them to enter the stables first. Hannah stopped and met his gaze. "Thank you for keeping your word. That's a novelty in my world."

"I'm sorry to hear that." His eyes skimmed over her. "You said you're comfortable around horses, right?"

"It's been a long time, but yes."

"How long is a long time?"

When she paused to think, a rope of melancholy tugged at her. There were very few things from her past that pulled at her heart. Her horse was one of those. But when she'd walked away from her grandmother, she'd walked away from everything her money could buy. "It's been more than seven years. A beautiful mare named Sage."

"What happened?"

"That's a story for another day." She stepped into the building, her boots echoing on the floor. The place was abuzz with activity. "Why are things so busy on a Saturday?"

He shrugged. "The usual. Lessons are scheduled Monday through Saturday. Most of the kids and staff sign up for recreational rides, as well."

She offered a small nod.

"I manage the equestrian center located on each ranch. We house over twenty ranch horses, plus those owned by the staff."

"That's a lot of horses and a lot of work," Hannah said. Her grandmother hired a team of grooms for her stables.

"The kids muck and groom as part of their daily chores."

"I'm sure that's helpful, but someone has to manage the entire program, including veterinarian visits, feed, supplies and the day-to-day issues."

He stared at her, a flicker of surprise crossing his face.

"I worked for the manager at an equine clinic long ago," she admitted. "Which may come in handy as your assistant."

"So you said." He paused. "That starts on Monday." Tripp offered a dismissive nod, before he turned to her daughter. "Miss Clementine, would you like to ride today?"

"Oh, yes, please, Mr. Tripp. I've never been on a real horse." She cocked her head and pursed her mouth for a moment. "Do you have any pink horses?"

"We don't, but I have a nice horse named Grace who would like to be your friend."

"Okay."

Once again, Clementine's short legs skipped to catch up to Tripp. Hannah's jaw nearly dropped when her daughter put her little hand in Tripp's and followed him. Clementine was friendly by nature, but this…this was unusual.

As she followed, Hannah spotted the tack room next to an office with glass windows all around. The sign on the door read Tripp Walker, Manager. They stopped at the last stall on the left where a chalkboard on the outside of the stall had Grace printed in white letters.

"Do you want to introduce yourself and Clementine to Grace while I grab some equipment?" Tripp asked.

"Oh, yes. Sure," Hannah returned.

"Mommy," Clementine whispered. "I'm really going to ride a horse?"

"You are." Hannah knelt down next to her daughter. "It's very important that you follow all of Mr. Walker's instructions today."

Clementine gave a solemn nod and then frowned. "His name is Mr. Tripp, Momma."

"Mr. Tripp." Hannah barely resisted rolling her eyes. "I'm going to lift you up so you can pet the horse's nose. Talk to her and say hello. Be very gentle."

Clementine reached toward Grace without hesitation. She stroked the animal's chestnut nose, her fingers lingering on the white patch of her forehead. "Hi,

Miss Grace. My name is Clementine," she soothed, like an old pro.

The animal gave a nicker and nudged at Clementine's hand.

Clementine's eyes popped wide, and she giggled. "Momma, she likes me."

"Why wouldn't she?" Tripp asked from behind them. He held a saddle, a blanket and a currycomb. "Come on, we'll get Grace ready to ride and I'll take you both for a little walk."

"Oh, I hate to take you away from your work," Hannah said. "I can do that."

He looked at her and seemed to be searching for a response. "Sometimes, I like to be taken away from my work."

"We've already imposed," Hannah protested.

Tripp cleared his throat. "Ma'am, there's a liability issue here."

"But I'm about to be an employee." She paused. "At least temporarily."

"Monday. After you fill out the paperwork and such on Monday, you'll be official and all."

Hannah swallowed and stepped back. "So I have to trust you with my daughter for now?"

"Yes, ma'am. You can watch from outside the corral."

Could she trust Tripp Walker with that which was most precious to her? Clementine was the reason she'd been on the run for the past nearly seven years. Leaving Colorado, she knew that their running had come to an end and that eventually, she'd have to trust someone. Maybe Big Heart Ranch was the place to start. After all, this ranch was all about trust and second chances, wasn't it?

She met Tripp Walker's steady gaze and nodded. "Okay."

* * *

Tripp lifted a grinning Clementine from the saddle and set her on the ground in the stables.

"How'd the ride go?" Rue asked as she entered the building.

"This little cowgirl is a natural," he said.

"I expected as much." Rue turned to Hannah. "I've got some friends to visit over at the chicken coop. Mrs. Carmody and the rest of the girls. I thought Clementine might like to join me. Would that be all right with you, Hannah?"

"I, um…" Hannah blinked, eyes wide, obviously caught off guard.

"Oh, yes. Please, Momma. It will be all right. I'll be good." Clementine's brown eyes begged as loud as her entreaty.

Tripp narrowed his gaze. The single mother didn't like to be separated from her baby. Had he misjudged her? Time would tell.

Hannah nodded and offered Rue a shaky smile. "Sure, okay."

When Tripp led Grace to her stall, Hannah followed. She cleared her throat. "I'll untack the horse. It's the least I can do, and clearly, Grace is no threat."

He glanced from Grace to Hannah and nodded his approval. "Let me know if you need anything." Tripp turned and headed to his office. "I've got to make a few calls."

Tripp settled into his desk chair and stared at his cell phone. He wrestled the merits of an idea brewing in the back of his mind and finally punched in the number.

A moment later, the sound of boots pounding through the stables could be heard. Dutch Stevens planted himself outside Tripp's office and knocked on the open door with his fist. The old cowboy pushed his ancient straw cowboy hat to the back of his head and stroked his gray mustache. "I need some help outside."

"Give me a minute."

"A minute? I don't have a minute. I've got a mean horse you bought who's trying to bust out of the trailer. What I need is another hand."

Though Tripp stood and kicked the office door closed with the toe of his boot, he could still hear Dutch griping through the glass as his cell connected.

"Hello?" the raspy voice on the phone said into Tripp's ear.

"Slats, this is Walker over at Big Heart Ranch. I need a favor."

"Guess I owe you a few, don't I?" Slats Milburn returned.

"I need a discreet background check."

"I'm always discreet."

"Good to know." He took a deep breath. "The name is Hannah Vincent."

Tripp swiveled his chair in time to see Hannah and Dutch talking outside Grace's stall. His trouble radar began to sound when Hannah tossed her sweater onto a wall peg and followed Dutch outside.

A moment later, a loud crash and bang of metal filled the stables, echoing over the noise of the riders and horses. Staff and children raced down the center aisle and poured into the sunlight to see what was going on.

"I gotta go. I'll text you the details." Tripp dropped the phone on his desk and wove past people crowded in the stable doorway.

Outside in the gravel parking area, Hannah Vincent lay on the ground with her posterior in a mud puddle while Dutch struggled to lead a rambunctious horse to the corral. Tripp stepped up to the horse, whose ears were snapped forward, his head up and the whites of his eyes bright as he whinnied in protest.

"What happened?" Tripp demanded.

Dutch grimaced. "Rowdy here kicked open the trailer same time I was opening the door. Horse exploded out of there. Door flew open and Miss Hannah went flying."

Hannah blinked and sat up. She shoved her dark hair from her eyes and brushed red dirt from her hands. "Sorry, I wasn't much help, Dutch."

"Aw, not your fault."

Tripp moved to Hannah's side, belatedly remembering that the woman was pregnant. When he did, it was a punch to his gut. "What were you thinking?" The words came out sharper than he intended.

"I said I'm fine," she answered.

Tripp and Dutch stood over Hannah, each offering a hand and helping her to her feet.

Dutch chuckled. "Never seen anyone go flying like that before."

"Yeah. We'll talk about that later," Tripp growled. He moved near the excited horse and spoke in soothing tones before he moved closer and started scratching and petting around the withers. As the horse stilled, Tripp rubbed him between the eyes. "It's going to be okay, buddy."

Tripp handed the horse off to a wrangler and turned back to Hannah.

"Got a few scratches on your arm, Hannah," Dutch said. The old cowboy grimaced, his eyes filled with concern. "That's my fault. I'm sorry."

She raised her arms and sure enough, gravel and dirt were embedded in scratches on the backside of her right forearm. Tripp cringed at the sight. She'd gotten hurt on his watch.

"I'm okay," Hannah repeated firmly. She slapped at her backside and straightened her blouse.

"We'll let Rue decide that," Tripp said. "She's the staff doctor. For now, we can clean it up and put on a little antiseptic ointment." He gave a curt nod toward the stables.

"Your concern is overwhelming," Hannah murmured drily as she followed him.

"Rinse your arm in the sink over there." Tripp cocked his head to the right. "Then come into my office. I have a first aid kit."

Minutes later, Hannah sat in Tripp's office staring at the wall as she held her arm up.

"What's that?" she asked.

He removed the cover from the antibiotic ointment and glanced up at the wall. She was staring at the poster for the 100-Day Mustang Challenge.

"Just what it says. One hundred days to gentle, halter break, saddle train, and build trust with a horse."

"Do you get to keep the horse when you're done?"

"Nope. End of the hundred days there's big grand finale competition and the animals are auctioned off by the Bureau of Land Management."

"So what's the point?"

"It's for a good cause. Re-homing mustangs, raising money to start the process all over again."

"All good, but that's it?" Hannah said.

"Braggin' rights. To say you've done it."

"And have you? Done it before?"

"No time." He shrugged. "Been on my bucket list for a while."

"What's the prize money for something like that?" she asked.

"This year, fifty grand."

Her eyes rounded. "That could buy a lot of buckets."

"Lift your arm," he said.

She complied, and he examined the abrasion. When he shifted his gaze sideways, he could see her long lashes resting on her flushed cheeks. Hannah's full mouth was set in a tight line as he applied the ointment. Tripp worked to gentle his touch, reminding himself it didn't matter how long her lashes were or how smooth her skin.

Except, the truth was, something about Hannah Vincent made him think about and feel things he hadn't considered in a long time. He quickly gave himself a reality check. Hannah's character was still under question. If the woman had secrets, Slats would find out exactly what they were.

Tripp's gaze wandered to the sweet curve of Hannah's neck. He glanced away, praying that Slats would be quick with his research.

And what if Hannah is as innocent as she appears? Tripp shot back at the errant thought, telling himself that the truth was, beautiful women didn't look twice at scarred men. They went for the pretty guys like Travis.

He wrapped Hannah's arm with gauze and taped the edges before stepping clear and putting plenty of space between them. "All done. Rue can check your arm when she and Clementine get back."

Hannah raised her arm and assessed his work. "Thank you."

"No problem," he said with a quick glance. Before he was able to look away, she met his gaze.

"Why do you keep looking at me like I'm a particularly annoying bug on your windshield?" she asked quietly.

"Didn't notice that I was." He sat down in his chair and put the ointment in the first aid kit, feigning nonchalance at her challenge.

"I'm not planning to sue you for a little scratch on my arm, so you can relax."

He was silent, knowing that she was spoiling for a fight.

"You've got something on your mind," Hannah continued. "You have since I arrived." She eyed him up and down. "You don't look like someone who plays games, so maybe you should just spit it out."

Tripp leaned back in his chair and crossed his arms. He prided himself on being a man of few words, but the woman was a burr under his saddle and for the first time in a long time, he couldn't keep his mouth shut.

"I keep asking myself what was so important that you had to risk yourself and your daughter in a storm yesterday and how a smart woman like yourself ran out of gas."

"I bought the car in Denver. Turns out the gas gauge sticks at times. Usually at the wrong times. Like Friday."

He gave a slow, considering nod.

"As for the other…do you have family?" She didn't wait for a response but plowed right ahead. "I found out forty-eight hours ago that I might. That was enough to put me on I-70 at noon on a Thursday headed to Oklahoma. Believe it or not, and I imagine you will choose not to, I was unaware that I was in the path of a tornado."

Tripp didn't know what to say to the outburst. But it didn't matter because Hannah Vincent wasn't done yet.

"It's clear you're determined to think the worst of me, Mr. Walker. It's a good thing I don't answer to you."

"You will," he murmured. "Come Monday."

When her face paled, remorse poked him in the chest. Now he'd gone and done it. Acted like a mule.

Why was this particular woman so good at pushing buttons he didn't even know he still had available to push? He stood and cleared his throat. "Excuse me. I've got work to do." Tripp felt her gaze staring him down as he left the office, but he had to get out of there before he shoved both of his boots in his mouth and discovered a perfect fit.

Chapter Three

Hannah slipped from her seat in a back row pew of the Timber Community Church the minute Pastor Parr dismissed the service. She'd barely taken a step when she ran into a wall of muscle and her Bible fell from her hands to the carpeted floor of the chapel. Stunned, she found herself inches from Tripp Walker as he scooped up the good book and offered it to her.

Accepting the tome from the lean cowboy, she stepped back and brushed an imaginary wrinkle from her simple cap sleeve lavender dress while avoiding eye contact. She would not notice his clean-shaven face, nor how blue his eyes were in that teal chambray shirt and navy tie.

"Thank you," she murmured. Without another word, she hurried past him to the church nursery hall to fetch Clementine.

Eyes on the room numbers, Hannah walked slowly down the long hall until she found Clementine's class. In the doorway of the next classroom, Lucy Maxwell Harris stood with a baby in her arms, herding three identical children into the hall. The triplets waved construction paper with colorful paintings and all jabbered at the same time.

Lucy looked up and her gaze met Hannah's. Her face lit up, and she seemed genuinely pleased at the encounter. "Hannah! Good to see you."

Hannah smiled at the unexpected welcome.

"How's your arm? I heard about Rowdy."

"A scratch. I've been upgraded from critical to a small bandage."

"That's good," Lucy returned.

"This is your family?" Hannah asked, eager to change the subject.

"It is." Lucy put a hand on the heads of each of the tow-headed children, one at a time. "Dub, Eva and Ann. They're seven now." Then she smiled down at the dark-haired baby with the sweet curls. "This is Daniel."

"Your family is precious." The words couldn't be any truer. Love radiated from the children's faces to their mother. "How old is Daniel?"

"Five months old this week." Lucy pressed a soft kiss to the infant's forehead. "Born on Christmas."

A Christmas baby. Like Hannah's baby would be, perhaps.

"Would you and your daughter like to join us for lunch?" Lucy asked. "Emma cooks on Sundays."

"I, um… That's very generous of you." Hannah stumbled over her words, surprised at the offer. "Clementine and I have plans. But thank you."

They did have plans, though in truth, until she could prove she was family she was an outsider and didn't want to be an interloper, as well. Besides, Tripp might be there and she'd had her quota of disapproving glances for the week.

"Where are we going, Momma?" Clementine asked once they were in the car headed to downtown Timber.

"It's Sunday, sweetie."

Clementine's eyes lit up.

The very least she could do for her daughter was maintain some semblance of routine over the last few weeks since they left Missouri. Sundays were for church and a special meal together. They'd kept that tradition while in Colorado and would continue here in Oklahoma.

"Pancakes?" Clementine asked with a hopeful lift of her brows.

"Whatever my girl wants." When they stopped at a light, Hannah reached into the back seat to straighten the pink bow in her daughter's hair.

"With whipped cream?"

"Of course."

Hannah passed the Timber Diner on Main Street and searched for a parking spot, finally pulling in outside the Timber Daily Gazette, which was closed.

A smiling server met them as they slid into a booth in the diner. "Coffee, ma'am?" the young woman asked.

"Decaf, please."

The server placed crayons and a paper placemat to color in front of Clementine. "And for you, miss?"

"Strawberry pancakes with whipped cream, please," Clementine said.

Hannah glanced around as her daughter examined the crayons. The view from the booth was limited. *We could have sat at a table.* The thought made her smile. No more hiding from whatever private detective her grandmother had hired. She was free.

"What did you do in Sunday school class, Clemmie?"

"I showed you my picture." Her daughter concentrated on coloring without looking up.

"Yes, and it's a beautiful picture of a pink horse and a house."

"No, Momma. That's Big Heart Ranch where my pink horse lives and so do I. Forever and ever."

Forever and ever. But only if the DNA test showed they were Maxwells.

She looked up and met the gaze of a tall, thin cowboy she didn't recognize. At least not from Big Heart Ranch. He stared first at her and then at Clementine. When the man realized she was looking back, he eased from the counter stool and headed out the door. Hannah shivered, offering up self-talk. *Nothing to worry about. Those days are gone. Just a coincidence our gazes met.*

When their server slid their plates in front of them, Hannah released the worrisome thoughts and took Clementine's hand for a mealtime prayer.

Hannah placed her napkin on her lap and tried to relax as her daughter dug right in.

"Good pancakes," Clementine mumbled.

"Sweetie, don't talk while you're chewing." She reached for a napkin and swiped at the whipped cream on her daughter's face.

Outside the window, budding tree branches reached for the Oklahoma blue sky where the spring sun peeked out from the clouds.

The clatter of silverware hitting the floor had Hannah turning her head back to the table. Clementine squirmed off the bench to retrieve a fork from the ground. She stood and pointed with the utensil. "Look, Momma. Mr. Tripp."

Hannah cringed as several patrons turned at the outburst. "Oh, sweetie, put down that fork. It's not polite to point."

Timber, Oklahoma, wasn't a big town, yet it still seemed odd that she wasn't able to go a day without running into Tripp Walker. Hannah dared to look up to confirm her daughter's comment. Yes, the cowboy's dusty boots were taking him across the room toward their booth. He'd changed into Levi's and a plaid Western shirt, but failed to look any less handsome and intimidating.

"Made it to church and to town, so I guess that means your car is still doing okay," Tripp said.

"Yes. Thank you for…" She raised her bandaged arm. "You know."

He pushed his hat to the back of his head with a finger and nodded.

"Did you eat pancakes, too, Mr. Tripp?" Clementine asked.

Hannah shot her daughter the *behave yourself* glance, willing the child not to embarrass her further.

"I did. I always have pancakes on Sunday," he returned. "Just like you are."

Clementine's face lit up at the words.

"You don't have family dinner with the Maxwells?" Hannah asked. The words were out of her mouth before she could take them back. What was she thinking asking such a personal question? It was none of her business, nor her matter to consider.

"Nothing better than a little alone time one day a week," he said without further explanation.

"You don't spend Sundays with family?" Oh, she was really on a roll now. Her mouth was clearly in gear and bypassing her brain. And did she imagine it, or did he tense at the question?

Tripp stared out the window. "No, ma'am." The cowboy blinked and his gaze returned to the table, moving from Hannah to Clementine. "I wanted to apologize for being a bit harsh yesterday."

"I, um…" Hannah nearly fell out of her seat at the unexpected admission. A suitable response failed her.

Tripp tipped his hat and turned. "You two have a nice day."

"Bye, Mr. Tripp," Clementine murmured between bites.

"Bye, Miss Clementine," he said as his long strides carried him away as quickly as he had appeared.

What just happened? Hannah sat back and did a mental play-by-play of the situation while her daughter finished off her meal, but minutes later, she still remained confused by the cowboy's hot and cold attitude.

When Clementine inched a pudgy finger onto her plate to wipe up the remaining syrup, Hannah flagged down the server as she passed by their booth.

"Ma'am, do you need more coffee?" the young woman asked.

"No, thank you. We're done, and my daughter gives your pancakes a thumbs-up."

"That's what we like to hear." The server grinned as she picked up their dishes.

"May I have the check?" Hannah asked.

"Oh, Mr. Walker paid for your meal and left me a generous tip." She smiled. "Y'all have a blessed Sunday."

Stunned, Hannah tried to wrap her mind around the fact that Tripp Walker paid for their brunch as she pulled a wet wipe from her purse and washed Clementine's sticky fingers.

"Mommy, I'm clean," Clementine declared.

"So you are, Clemmie."

Confused, Hannah glanced up and down the side-walk for the cowboy as they headed to their car. She didn't know what to make of the gesture. Did he think she needed a handout? She'd taken care of herself and her daughter for many years.

It was time to put Mr. Tripp Walker in his place. Hannah Vincent didn't need help, nor did she want any handouts.

"This is the day that the Lord has made," Tripp said as he unlocked the door to his office on Monday morning and turned on the lights.

Sunday's sermon had been about compassion and second chances. Apparently, the good Lord thought he needed to review. And He was right. Tripp repented while kneeling in the pew and followed through with an apology to Hannah at the diner.

Though he still wasn't thrilled about working in proximity with Hannah Vincent, he'd manage until further notice or Slats provided him with information that changed the situation.

Tripp grimaced, not certain contacting the private investigator was a wise move or fell in line with Pastor Parr's sermon goals. It was a little late for regrets, he reminded himself while absently rubbing his hand over the scar on his face. Slats informed him yesterday as they crossed paths outside the diner that he was on the job. Tripp could only pray that Hannah came up smelling like an Oklahoma rose.

He glanced at the clock and then his cramped office. Dutch had helped him move a desk and computer into the room for Hannah. It was in the opposite corner from his own desk and faced the window.

That way she could see into the stables…at least, that was his rationalization of the situation. In truth, he didn't need to be staring at the woman eight hours a day even if she did have long eyelashes and a pretty face. Not that he'd ever admit that to anyone but his horse.

Tripp turned at a knock on the door.

Hannah stood in the doorway looking like someone stole her puppy. "Sorry I'm late. It was Clementine's first day in daycare."

"First day? Like, ever? Or just here at the ranch?"

"Ever, except for the church nursery on Sundays. We've always been together."

"What about when you worked?"

"I always found a way to keep her with me."

"Overprotective?"

"Yes."

"So how's she doing?"

Hannah bit her lip. "Clementine is fine. It's her mother who's having adjustment issues."

"You can check on her during the day, if that will help."

Her eyes rounded with cautious hope. "That would be okay with you?"

He nodded. "Of course."

"Thank you."

They stood awkwardly for a few seconds before he remembered what he was supposed to do.

"That's your desk," he finally said. "I've put your tentative schedule on top. When I'm here, you're here. That means basically we work one Saturday a month. The staff alternate working Saturdays. Chores are scheduled for Sunday, but everyone is expected to be in church. Those are ranch rules."

Hannah offered a short nod as she stepped hesitantly

into the office, put her purse in the bottom desk drawer and sat down. She turned to him. "Mr. Walker, thank you for picking up our tab yesterday, but it was wholly unnecessary."

Her expression tacked the word *unwanted* onto the end of her spiel.

"I'm not looking for handouts," she continued.

"First, I'm Tripp. Not Mr. Walker." He tipped back his tan cowboy hat on his head and then crossed his arms. "Second, there's no need to get offended. I was paying it forward."

"Paying it forward?"

"Yeah. Don't overthink the situation."

She opened her mouth and then closed it again.

"Did you complete the paperwork at human resources?" he asked.

"Yes. They fingerprinted me, and I have my security pass for the gate. I'm ready to go, pending the results of the background check."

"Your temporary password and login information are on that paper on the desk. You have an appointment with Iris, Lucy's admin, over at the administration building this afternoon. She'll walk you through the programs we use on the ranch, payroll, vendor orders and scheduling."

"Oh, I thought you would…"

"You don't want me teaching you anything that has to do with a computer. I type with two fingers and I barely speak the language."

Hannah nodded.

"I'll show you around the boys' ranch stables today and tomorrow we'll go over to the girls' ranch."

"'Scuse me, Tripp. Got a problem with Rowdy again.

He's holding his hoof off the ground, and he won't let me near him."

He looked to Hannah. "We can do the tour later."

"Of course."

Rowdy, again. The horse was a stout nine-year-old Sorrel gelding with a flaxen mane and long, flowing flaxen tail. Perfect for the riding program…or so he'd thought. Besides the horse's fear of trailers, clearly something had happened since Tripp first saw the horse and now. Rowdy moved back with each step Tripp made toward him.

"Easy, boy. Easy."

When he got close enough to touch him, Tripp ran a hand over his withers, slowly massaging back and forth, until the horse was relaxed. Finally, he eased his hand toward the animal's affected leg, inching closer, slowly and patiently. He moved toward the horse's ankle, gaining trust until Rowdy was willing to let him hold his foot and examine the hoof.

"Stone in here. I'm guessing he came over to us like that. It's festered. He'll need the vet and the farrier."

"They don't call him the horse whisperer for nothing," Dutch said with a nod to Hannah.

"That's what they call him?" Hannah asked.

"Yep."

"Don't listen to that horse whisperer malarkey. What I do is called common sense," Tripp said as he strode past them toward the stables.

"Where are you going?" Dutch hollered after him.

"To call the vet."

Hannah walked up and down the equine center looking into stalls as Tripp talked to the vet. By the time his conversation was completed and he was back at his desk, she had moved into the office, sat at her desk and logged into the computer.

"The sign-up deadline for that mustang competition is coming up," she murmured.

Tripp looked up from his calendar. "What?" A glance at Hannah's computer screen told him she was searching the 100-Day Mustang Challenge site. The woman was a bulldog with a bone.

"You know." Hannah pointed to the poster on the wall.

"I told you. I have a full-time commitment to the ranch." He didn't even attempt to hold the annoyance from his voice.

"I'll help you."

"You?" He shook his head at her offer. "And what makes you think you can help me enough that I'll have time to train a mustang?"

"I looked at your schedule on the wall outside. There isn't anything on that list that I can't do."

"You're pregnant."

"Pregnant is not a terminal disease, and I don't need to ride a horse to help you. I saw that ute out there. That'll work. I mentioned that I have an extensive background with horses. I worked in children's camps and equine clinics when I was a teenager and when I was in college."

"So you keep saying." Tripp narrowed his eyes as he tried to figure the woman out. "What exactly did you go to college for?"

"Business administration with a minor in accounting."

"Why?"

"My grandmother was paying."

He continued to stare. The woman was a puzzle.

"Why aren't you working as a bookkeeper or accountant then?"

"Because childcare is expensive."

"College isn't?"

"I've already explained that."

Tripp frowned. Yeah, and his gut told him something was not right with Hannah's explanation. Hopefully, Slats would be able to sort it out.

"Let me get this straight. A woman with a degree in business, who works as a cook, is telling me how to run my equine facility and the mustang challenge?"

"Who told you I work as a cook?"

"You mentioned it during your meeting with the Maxwells last Friday."

"Oh." Hannah exhaled. "My point is that I think you should consider doing the 100-Day Mustang Challenge."

"Why?"

"Is that the only word you know?"

"Maybe so." He shrugged.

"You should enter because you can do it and because the purse is fifty thousand dollars."

"Money isn't high on my priority list."

"That's why you have that poster on the wall?"

"I like the idea of rehoming the animal." He gave a slow shake of his head. "But you and I working together? It'd never work. We rub each other the wrong way."

Hannah's brows shot up and her eyes rounded. "That's your issue, not mine. And in case you haven't noticed, we're already working together."

A knock on the door had both of them turning to see Travis Maxwell. "What are you two talking about?"

"The 100-Day Mustang Challenge," Hannah said.

"*We* weren't talking. She was."

"You finally going to do it, Tripp?" Travis offered an enthusiastic grin.

"One of these days," he groused. Because he sure wasn't going to let a bossy thing like Hannah Vincent push him into anything.

"Why not now?" Travis asked.

"'Cause I don't have anything to prove. I train horses all the time."

"Tripp, you're not going to stay with us forever. I know that. This might be a good way to get your name out there and get you on your way to your own horse training facility. You used to talk about doing that all the time."

Tripp frowned, his mind taking a cautious detour to consider Travis's words. *Used to* was a long time ago. What had happened to his dreams along the way?

"I don't know," Tripp finally said.

"Come on. I know I could talk Lucy into the idea. Let Big Heart Ranch help you. You've helped us. You worked for us when we could barely pay you."

"Where would we put a wild horse?"

"We'll clear the old barn and set up a dedicated round pen for training."

"And the prize money?" Tripp asked.

Travis raised his hands. "Hey, that's all yours. The ranch is a charity. We won't touch your winnings."

Silence stretched for moments as Tripp battled with the idea of change. The *terrifying* idea of change. His life was a steady, predictable ride right now. Why look for trouble?

"I'll think about it," he finally said.

"Think hard. When the door opens, you have to walk through. Big Heart Ranch didn't get to be where it is without us stepping out in faith."

Tripp cleared his throat, eager to change the topic. He met Travis's gaze head-on. "Did you have something on your mind when you stopped by?"

"I came to tell Hannah that Lucy scheduled an appointment with the lab in Tulsa for them two weeks from now. Soonest she could fit it in. Lucy's schedule is tight this time of year."

"Why can't you or Emma go to the lab with her?" Tripp asked.

"I can't go because female-to-female DNA comparison yields a more accurate result. Emma can't go because Lucy is a helicopter sister. She still thinks she's in charge of me and Emma."

"I guess so," Tripp murmured.

"Thank you," Hannah said. When Travis left, she turned to Tripp again. "That was a confirmation."

"A what?"

"A confirmation. You know, a sign that you should enter the challenge."

Tripp looked her up and down. The woman was a sassy thing for a stranger who'd only arrived a few days ago.

"You don't even know if you'll be here in one hundred days," he returned.

Though her eyes said she was dumbstruck by his bold statement, her mouth kept moving. "You don't believe I'm related to the Maxwells, do you?"

Tripp raised both hands. "I don't know what to believe." Though he tried not to judge, there was a part of him that had already stamped the woman's card and dismissed her.

"I am, and I'm willing to stick around to find out if it will help Clementine."

"Help Clementine?"

Hannah offered a shrug. "We could use a little nest egg to start over."

"The prize money?"

"Sure. Why not? If I make it possible for you to train, maybe it would be worth some of the purse." The flush of her cheeks told him that her words were all bravado.

"What makes you think I'm going to win?" Tripp asked.

"I've seen you with the horses." She paused. "I know a winner when I see one."

He nearly laughed aloud. "So what kind of split are we talking about here?" he asked.

"Fifty-fifty."

Tripp released a scoffing sound. "In your dreams, lady. I'm the trainer and I'm paying for fees and feed and everything else out of my pocket."

"Sixty-forty?"

"More like seventy-thirty, and you have a deal." The words slipped from his mouth before he could take them back. What was he thinking, making a pact with a pregnant single mother who might very well prove to be a seasoned con artist? His mouth hadn't run off on him in years. Yet here he was, with his good sense galloping away.

"I, um…"

Despite his misstep, Hannah seemed reluctant to commit, and that stuck in his craw. Was she having second thoughts about his ability to win the challenge?

"What's the problem?" he asked. "Your bravado seems to be fading the closer it gets to the chute."

"Seventy-thirty?" She shook her head in disagreement.

"Are you telling me that you couldn't start over with

fifteen thousand dollars? If you can't, then you're doing it all wrong, my friend."

"We aren't friends," Hannah said. Then she stood and walked over to his desk. She offered him her hand, and he stared at it for a moment before accepting the handshake.

"Deal," she said.

Tripp stared at her small hand in his.

The day had started off like any other. In a heartbeat, everything was sideways. He'd agreed to the 100-Day Mustang Challenge and was seriously thinking about a future that didn't include the Maxwells.

Was he ready to move on from Big Heart to start his own business? The thought left him as nervous as a heifer about to give birth. Tripp offered a silent prayer, knowing this was going to take a real step of faith and no doubt bigger boots than he had on.

Chapter Four

"I don't understand why Clementine couldn't come with us," Hannah said. About now, she was feeling like her daughter on the downside of a temper tantrum. Being stuck in a truck cab with Tripp Walker for three hours and seven minutes one way might be the reason.

She stared out the passenger window of Tripp's pickup at the Oklahoma countryside. Today the view had easily earned the name Green Country. Only minutes ago, cedar elm and bald cypress trees graced the emerald green lawns of residential properties they passed when they detoured from the highway to a small town for beverages and a rest stop.

Tripp adjusted his sunglasses and rolled down his window a bit to let in the morning breeze. "The Bureau of Land Management station in Pauls Valley is not a place for children."

"If this is because of that incident with the feed yesterday, I said it was an accident. We've had a discussion about going into the stalls alone," Hannah protested. "Clementine understands."

Tripp held up a hand. "Not insulting your child, Momma. She's as smart as a dozen five-year-olds put together. Most kids are naturally curious. Your daughter is all that ratcheted up to Mach four."

Hannah grudgingly admitted that even though he'd only known Clementine a week, his assessment was spot-on.

He shot her a sideways glance. "You didn't have to come with me."

"Of course I did. This is my future. I'm so excited I could barely sleep last night."

"Then try to relax. Clementine is having a great time with Lucy's triplets."

"Lucy has four children already."

"She loves kids. More importantly, everyone loves Clementine."

"They do?" Hannah's spirits lifted at the unexpected words.

"Yeah. You haven't noticed? Your daughter brings out a smile wherever she goes."

"Thank you," Hannah said softly. She glanced at the cowboy out of the corner of her eye. "That was a really nice thing to say."

"Wasn't trying to be nice. Those are the facts." Tripp offered his usual shrug as he checked both ways before easing back onto Interstate 35. When the truck hit a bump, the empty horse trailer behind them rattled. "Besides, six hours round-trip is no fun for a kid."

Hannah conceded that he was right on that count as well, though being without her daughter for this long was new territory and a bit scary. Maybe she was a helicopter mother, but for good reason. She'd been raised by a series of nannies and a judgmental grandmother. Hannah was determined Clementine would know her mother and feel unconditionally loved at all times.

After the first hour, Hannah got used to the silence

that stretched between her and Tripp in the truck, and she relaxed. He apparently liked it quiet as much as she did. The radio was off and whenever she sneaked a peek at his profile, she found him focused on the road as if thinking very hard.

What was going on in the man's head? It was hard to say, and she'd already figured out that he wasn't going to give her more words than absolutely necessary.

She peeked at his profile again. With his hat tipped back and his eyes locked on the road, he seemed unnecessarily attractive. Perhaps more so because he had little regard for superficial things like appearances.

"I hope we find a good horse," Hannah finally spoke into the silent truck cab.

"Yeah, except that's not how it works. You get what you get."

"What do you mean? I thought we'd be able to pick the horse we spend one hundred days training."

"Not unless we participate in the auction." He shook his head. "And that's not going to happen. Doesn't make sense to spend money bidding on a horse that's going to be auctioned off again in one hundred days. Nope. We'll do things like everyone else. What we get is what we train. That's the real challenge."

"That certainly doesn't seem fair."

"It's not about fair." He shot her a quick look. "And I'm guessing by now you realize life isn't fair."

She pulled her denim jacket close and frowned. "It doesn't mean I have to like it."

"This challenge is all about the big picture. Come September, the horses will be adopted."

Cocking her head, she turned to look at him. "How many is that, exactly?"

"Close to three thousand."

Hannah leaned back against the seat. "I had no idea."

"There are about sixty thousand horses being held in Bureau of Land Management facilities across the United States."

Stunned, Hannah opened her mouth and closed it again.

"Truth is, I'm glad you lassoed me into this challenge. It's about time I gave back."

"Really?"

"Yeah." Once again, he looked at her. "Don't read anything into that."

"No. Of course not." Hannah directed her gaze out the window at the highway signs. *Chickasha. Anadarko. Shawnee. Seminole.*

"Native American names," she murmured.

"What?" His gaze followed hers to the signs. "Yeah. Chickasha, Shawnee and Seminole are tribal names. Anadarko is headquarters for a good many tribal nations."

"Have you lived around here all your life?"

Tripp nodded. "Rumor has it that my great-grandfather on my mother's side was from the Osage Nation."

"Rumor?"

"I don't have any family left to verify that information."

"Oh. I'm so sorry." She lifted a hand in gesture. "I was just making conversation. I didn't mean any offense."

"Why would I be offended?"

"I just thought… Never mind." Hannah paused. "I don't have any family, either."

"No one at all?"

"No," she said. "My grandmother raised me."

"And you drove all the way here from Colorado."

Hannah stiffened at the question. How many times did she have to explain before he believed her? "Actually, I drove all the way from Missouri by way of Colorado. They're holding my job in case I decide to come back."

"I guess you were pretty good if they're holding your job. What did you do? Some kind of cook, right?"

"Yes. I was the head cook at a very popular twenty-four-hour diner in Dripping Falls, Missouri." She glanced at him. "And yes, I am a really good cook. Plus, I was in great demand during tax season for my mathematical skills."

He said nothing for minutes, clearly not impressed by her résumé. Yes, right, she wasn't, either. She had graduated from an Ivy League school at the top of her class so she could be a short-order cook. A total waste of time, energy and tuition.

"Dripping Falls," Tripp mused. "Population three thousand and twenty on a good day. Two stoplights and a one-way street around the center of town."

"How could you possibly know that?" Hannah asked. She was dismayed that he'd been checking on her.

"I caught a glimpse of your paperwork. Got curious and looked it up." He spared her a glance, clearly holding back a smile. "Seriously? Dripping Falls?"

"Despite the name, it's a very nice town."

He nodded as though considering her words. "You're a jill-of-all-trades, aren't you?"

"I suppose that's one way of looking at it. I have a daughter to consider so I'll do whatever I have to do to make ends meet for her."

"Her daddy?"

"You certainly ask a lot of questions," Hannah shot back.

"Just making conversation. I guess that's a sore subject."

"Not at all. I have nothing to hide." She fiddled with the brass snap on her jacket. "Clementine doesn't really know her daddy well. His loss."

"That I can agree with," Tripp murmured.

A half a mile down the road, he turned on his signal and nodded his head toward the right.

Hannah read the sign at the entrance. Bureau of Land Management Horse and Burro Adoption Center. "This facility doesn't look like much," she observed.

"Twelve pastures and four hundred acres of land. They've got six hundred animals they're holding before they're moved east or west to adoption centers. Lots of controversy about the land and the animals that roam wild and free. But we're not getting into that today."

She glanced around. Several other rigs with trailers were parked in the facility parking area and a line of people had formed outside a small building.

"What do we do now?" Hannah asked.

"Pick up our registration packet over there and then they'll pull our horse for us."

"That's it?"

"That's it. I registered us for the challenge online."

"Us?" She blinked at the comment.

"Both of our names are on those forms." Tripp eased the truck into a parking spot and turned off the engine.

"I don't have any credentials."

"You were added as the assistant trainer, based on my recommendation."

"You don't even know me."

"Nope." He met her gaze before he jumped down from the cab. "So you better not prove me wrong and ruin my reputation."

"Yes, sir." Hannah carefully eased down from the truck before Tripp could come around and assist her.

Once Tripp locked the truck and headed toward the registration area, Hannah realized she'd have to walk twice as fast to keep up with his long strides.

The line moved quickly. They picked up their paperwork and moved over to the main corral where at least forty horses raced around the giant metal circular pen, grunting and whinnying. A few rambunctious ones kicked at the pole fencing and the sound of hooves hitting metal rang into the morning air. Beautiful animals, strong and filled with pride, waited restlessly for their futures to be decided.

Hannah stared at the sight for a long minute while Tripp handed his receipt with the horse's number to the cowboy manning the loading chute.

"You got a good one," the cowboy said with a laugh. "We nicknamed her Calamity Jane." He pointed to an animal with a copper-red coat and dark brown-and-copper mane, about fourteen hands, who edged closer to the gate latch. "That's her. Five-year-old sorrel mare. Good-natured animal."

"Calamity Jane? Why's that?" Hannah asked.

"Oh, she's smart. Too smart. Couple of times she tried to jump the fence."

"That's a ten-foot fence," Tripp said.

"*Tried* being the operative word." He chuckled. "Failing that, she got her mouth on the gate latch during the night. Given a little more time, I do believe she might have opened the pen."

"Calamity Jane," Tripp murmured with a smile.

"Yeah, she's something special." The cowboy nodded. "Back your rig up and we'll get her loaded."

Hannah guided Tripp with hand signals as he steered the trailer until the entire rig was backed up to the loading chute. She raised her palms, and the vehicle stopped.

Tripp got out, jumped the fence and unlatched the trailer, opening the doors wide before he jumped back out of the chute and away from the horses.

Hannah's gaze followed the cowboy in the holding pen as he encouraged Jane toward the narrow chute.

"Ya!" the cowboy called out, urging Calamity Jane toward the trailer.

For a moment the horse stopped as if in slow motion and turned to the left, the chocolate eyes searching. When her gaze connected with Hannah's, the mare moved closer to the fence. Hannah raised her hand, flat palm up. She was far enough back to stay safe, but her gesture caught the horse's attention. Jane sniffed curiously.

"Well, I'll be," the cowboy murmured. "I've never seen anything like that from these mustangs."

The horse blinked and then shook her head, tossing her mane back and forth as if breaking a spell.

"Ya. In you go," the cowboy said from his perch on the fence. The sound of hooves on the trailer floor told them Calamity Jane was tucked inside.

Tripp jumped forward to close the gate and latch everything securely. "Thanks," he said with a nod to the cowboy.

"Let me know how it goes," the cowboy said. "I meant what I said. I really have the feeling you've got something special there."

Something special. Hannah shivered. Exactly what she'd been praying for. A horse who needed her as much as she needed it.

"What are your plans?" Hannah turned to Tripp as she fastened her seat belt.

"Plans?" He adjusted his hat and put on his sunglasses.

"Training plans."

Tripp shrugged. "Ask the horse. I just show up. The rest is up to her."

"No. You can't mean that. You're a trainer. I imagine you've trained dozens of animals."

"More than dozens and generally, they trained me," he murmured with a lift of his brow.

"How can I help?"

"You can do all the administrative chores so I can train this horse. That's the deal."

"You put me down as co-trainer."

"Hannah, that was honorary. The challenge was your idea and I'm giving credit where credit is due. You're enabling me to train. Assistant trainer aside, I don't want to see you in the same pen or stall with that horse, ever."

"That's not your business..." She clamped her mouth shut before she could finish and allow an opening for Tripp to give her one of his lectures.

"You're pregnant. Don't do anything that could compromise your or your baby's health. That horse is wild and unpredictable, and you're not taking risks on my watch."

She offered a tortured sigh. Apparently, lecturing was on today's menu anyhow.

"I'm not going to ride." Hannah took a deep breath and crossed her arms. She had no intention of doing anything that would put this pregnancy at risk. At the same time, she wasn't going to let anyone, including her enigmatic boss, tell her what to do.

"You heard me. My stable. My rules."

"What exactly does that mean? You want me to sit at a desk all day?"

"It means you're going to do what you signed on for.

Keep the books, manage the schedule, order the supplies and answer the phone."

If Hannah bit her tongue any harder she was pretty sure she'd draw blood. But she'd learned a long time ago that it was a waste of time to go through when you could go around. If there was a way around the stubborn cowboy, well, she was just the gal to find that road.

Tripp downed the last of his coffee and opened the door of the bunkhouse.

May had turned to June in the blink of an eye, bringing with it warm temperatures and sunshine. At nearly six, the sun had managed to paint the sky in gold and burnt umber as it stretched sleepy fingers toward daylight.

He stepped out to the gravel yard, enjoying the quiet. When he turned the corner, a lone figure stood silhouetted at Calamity Jane's fence. Murmured words had the mare leaning closer.

Hannah.

She reached a hand through the fence to stroke the horse's mane.

Unbelievable. They brought Jane home on Tuesday and here it was Wednesday. Less than twenty-four hours and already she had bonded with the mare. Somehow between yesterday and this morning, Jane had figured out that touch was a good thing. Tripp wasn't certain who should be applauded: Hannah or the horse.

As Tripp got closer, Jane's ears perked, and she whinnied as if warning Hannah of his approach. Two females in cahoots. Just perfect.

Hannah whirled around to face him, pushing her dark waves back. "Did you see that?"

He was dumbstruck at the sweet expression she gave

him. A smile lit up her face all the way to her brown eyes, which fairly sparkled with happiness.

Tripp caught himself before he stumbled.

"Did you bring her a treat?" he asked.

Hannah laughed. "Excuse me. I do not bribe horses. Jane happens to appreciate me just the way I am."

"Is that so?" Tripp moved closer, resting his arms on a rung of the high pen fence. Jane raced around the circle, kicking up dirt and sand, the tilt of her head proud. There wasn't a more awesome sight to behold on all of Big Heart Ranch.

Overhead, a hawk circled in the clear powder blue sky, doing a lazy dip before he landed on the branches of a mighty elm tree.

"What are you going to do today?" Hannah asked, her voice eager and enthusiastic.

"I'll let her run the pen, get her used to me. Just like yesterday. She's committed to ignoring me. I'm committed to not letting her."

Hannah smiled. "She's watching you right now."

"Yeah. That's exactly what I want. She's a little jealous of all the attention I'm not giving her at this moment."

"Most trainers would force her to bend to their will."

"That's how either the horse or the trainer gets hurt. Though it's not my place to be critical, there are many right and wrong ways to train a horse." He paused. "I'll stick with what works for me."

"Can I help?"

Tripp kept his voice low, his eyes on Jane. "Are we going to have this same discussion every day?"

"There has to be something I can do."

"There is. May not seem like much, but having you in the office frees me up so I can take my time out here with our friend." He turned and met Hannah's gaze. "You are vital to the success of this challenge."

"Vital. That sounds very important." Her tone said she was being sarcastic again.

"Yeah. You do your job, and I'll do mine."

"Tripp, look." Hannah's attention was focused on the pen behind him.

He turned back in time to see the horse mouthing the gate latch and nearly opening it wide. Tripp chuckled. "I wouldn't have believed that if I hadn't seen it."

Pulling a bandana from his pocket, he tied the gate near the bottom. "This will do for now. I'll have Dutch add an extra latch."

"I wish Clementine could have seen that," Hannah said.

"Where is she?"

"Rue is going to bring her to daycare this morning. The doctor is going to do eye exams in the childcare classrooms today."

"You talked to Clementine about the horses, especially this one, right?"

"We had a chat, and she repeated the rules back to me."

He nodded. "The local vet, Trent Blaylock, will be by at nine or so this morning to check on a few issues. If you could follow him around with Dutch, I'd appreciate it. I'd like to work with Jane without interruptions around that time."

"Of course."

"All you have to do is make note of his recommendations and leave your notes on my desk. Trent is easy to work with."

"Will do." She paused. "Lucy asked me to help with a church fund-raiser she's working on."

"Okay?"

"That means I have to go to a meeting Friday morning. It's at the chow hall."

"Fine by me."

"Thank you. But, um, where is the chow hall again?"

"Here at the boys' ranch, right next to the administration building. It's the cafeteria."

"Got it."

Tripp left Hannah at the corral and headed to the stables. Flipping on the lights to his office, he sat down at his desk and blinked. He was a tidy man but things were tidier than usual. Hannah had left paperwork with sticky notes indicating his signature was needed. The May accounts had all been checked and verified and were ready to close out with checks sent.

A pang of guilt stabbed at him. He needed to call and tell Slats to back off. Except the cowboy was in Texas this week for a rodeo and probably not picking up his phone.

Still, he could leave a message.

Tripp looked around to be sure Hannah hadn't slipped into the stables.

He hit auto dial and to his surprise, the cowboy picked up.

"Slats, this is Tripp Walker."

"I was going to call you today."

"Yeah, well, I want to cancel that request. You know the one."

"There's something you ought to know first."

"Whatever it is, I don't want to know."

The woman worked for him; if there was something he needed to know, he'd find out himself. Hiring Slats had been a bad idea and for the first time in years, Tripp knew that he was dipping into dangerous territory. You hang around in low places, you become a low place.

He looked up when Hannah quietly stepped into the room and moved to her desk.

"Bill me and I'll drop a check in the mail."

Tripp didn't give Slats a chance to respond. He hit the end button, stood and tucked his phone in the back pocket of his jeans.

"I'll be with Jane if anything comes up."

"Yes, sir."

"*Sir* isn't necessary."

Hannah didn't look up from the spreadsheet on the computer screen. "My grandmother had her issues, but she taught me proper respect for my elders."

First Dutch and now Hannah. "I'm not that old," Tripp grumbled under his breath as he headed to Jane's pen. The sorrel mare followed Tripp around for two hours, stopping when he stopped and changing direction at his pleasure.

He put a light blanket on her back and she barely reacted. If he didn't know this horse was from the Bureau of Land Management he'd have never believed the fact. The horse was a lover, longing for affection and giving back the same.

"Whoa," he said with a pat to the mare's bare backside. "Good job, Jane."

Tripp looked up in time to see Dutch walking back to the stables alongside Rowdy.

"How's Rowdy doing?"

"Vet says he's ready to ride."

"Great, and how's he behaving?"

"Settled down some. I think this fella's going to fit right in."

"Great. Until we're sure of his temperament, keep him scheduled with the certified instructors only."

"You sure that's necessary?" Dutch asked.

"Something's not right yet," Tripp said. "Be careful with him. Jane here is less twitchy than Rowdy, and that's not a good sign."

"Will do, boss."

"Dutch, don't forget I need an extra latch for this gate."

"On my list. I'll be going to town this afternoon. Need anything else?"

"Check with Travis before you go."

"I already did. Won't be any flies on me today. Between you and Travis, I'm working from can to can't." Dutch paused then looked pointedly at Tripp before glancing around.

"Something on your mind?" Tripp asked.

Dutch stepped closer to the pen. "I'm not privy to all the information like you are, but I hear tell Hannah might be a Maxwell."

"How'd you squirrel that information?"

"I pestered Rue until she finally let it slip." Dutch shrugged. "I'd have to be half-dead and living under a rock not to figure something was up around this place. You getting an assistant and all was the kicker."

Tripp faced the weathered cowboy. "Did you just insult me?"

"Nope, just stating the facts. You're not exactly a social being, so you getting an assistant and signing up for the hundred-day challenge, well, it sure seemed the world must have been knocked off kilter a bit."

When Tripp offered a death stare, the weathered wrangler raised his hands.

"I tells it like I sees it."

"Lucy and Travis have been promising me an assistant for a long time. That's no secret." Tripp grabbed his lead rope from the fence and wrapped it up.

"And the challenge?" Dutch persisted.

"You don't expect me to stay here at Big Heart for the rest of my life, do you?"

"Why not? That's my plan. I figured it was yours, too."

Tripp stared at him. Did everyone think he was a fixture here at Big Heart? A man without dreams of his own? He shook his head. Maybe he'd done that to himself, put his dreams on the back burner because it was safer that way.

"I'm not a hundred years old, Dutch," he finally muttered. The words *like you* hung in the air between them.

The old cowboy frowned. "No need to be disparaging."

"You asked." Tripp checked Jane's feed bucket.

"So that's all you know about Hannah?" Dutch asked.

Tripp wordlessly stared him down. Dutch knew good and well that Tripp wouldn't tell him anything, even if he did know something. The wrangler couldn't keep a secret to save himself.

"That's what I figured you'd say," Dutch muttered.

"Everything go okay with the vet?" Tripp asked.

"Hannah and Trent are still in your office, jabbering."

"Jabbering?"

"Yeah. Don't know about what, but it looks serious. Those two are getting along like long-lost friends."

Tripp stepped into the stables. Sure enough, through the glass windows of his office he could see that Hannah seemed to be lecturing the vet. Trent nodded thoughtfully as though he hung on her every word.

Suddenly Trent smiled and offered Hannah a quick hug.

A strange emotion wrapped itself around Tripp. If he had any interest in Hannah, he might have suspected it was jealousy. Except that was a crazy notion. The last thing he needed in his life was a woman. If he did, it sure wouldn't be Hannah Vincent.

Not only was she trouble, but she was an opinionated, bossy woman. A single mother with more baggage than he had time to deal with and more on the way.

The vet met his gaze as he exited the offices. "Hey, Tripp. I don't know where you got Hannah, but she's a keeper."

Tripp nodded. A keeper? Confused, he turned.

When Hannah's gaze connected with his, her lips curved into a smile. A pink blush warmed her cheeks, and for the second time that morning he was hit with a jolt in his midsection. He quickly looked away.

"Looked like you and Trent hit it off," Tripp said as he sat down and fiddled with the papers on his desk.

"We did. He's a nice guy. Turns out we know a few of the same people. In Colorado, no less." A musing smile lit up her face.

"Trent's father is an Oklahoma senator," Tripp said, trying to connect the dots between Hannah and the blue blood family.

"I know," she said.

Dutch stuck his head in the door. "I'm headed into town now."

"Oh, Dutch, may I go with you? I got an email the supplies I ordered are in."

"Surely. I'll meet you at the ranch truck."

She turned and looked at Tripp. "I'll have the vet visit notes typed up and on your desk as soon as I get back."

"This afternoon is fine." Tripp glanced at the clock. "What about your lunch break?"

"Oh, I'll have a yogurt when I get back."

"Aren't you supposed to be eating for two?"

She frowned. "You're an obstetrician in your spare time?"

"Have you been to one lately?"

"It's on my list." She cocked her head and gave him a slow assessment. "Burr under your saddle?"

"Not that I know of."

She opened the bottom drawer of her desk and reached for her purse. "Maybe you're right about lunch. Today's the meat loaf special at the diner. I'll take Dutch with me."

"Great," Tripp muttered as she left. He'd been so rushed he hadn't even packed a lunch today, and he was pretty sure he'd memorized the contents of the mini-fridge. Opening the door, he stared. An apple and a jar of crunchy peanut butter stared back at him.

If he had more sense, he would have offered to take Dutch and Hannah out to eat himself. He reached for the apple. No one ever accused Tripp Walker of having too much sense.

Chapter Five

Hannah slid into a chair at the table in the chow hall on Friday morning. The combination cafeteria and gathering room for special events had enough long laminated picnic-like tables and chairs for the entire ranch. The walls were covered with framed, enlarged photographs of ranch events. Hannah spotted Tripp in more than one picture, always with the horses and the ranch children. Her heart did a little leap at the rare smile that had been captured in one particular photo. The man related to four-legged animals and kids. Adults, not so much. Why was that?

She glanced at the big schoolhouse clock and paced back and forth, becoming more and more nervous.

"Hannah! You're early."

Hannah turned at the oldest Maxwell's voice. Lucy's administrative assistant, Iris, trailed behind, talking on her cell phone while writing on a clipboard. Both wore red T-shirts bearing the Big Heart Ranch logo. "So glad you're here," Lucy continued.

"I'm happy to help, though I don't know what I can do." *And I have no clue why you would want me to help.*

"We need some fresh ideas and you're part of the

brainstorming process," Lucy said, clearly reading her mind. She put a folder on a table and sat down. Iris placed a legal pad next to Lucy and slipped into a chair.

"Sorry I'm late," Emma Maxwell Norman called as she pushed through the glass doors. "Meeting with the twins' teacher. They've been fighting over a boy in class."

Lucy chuckled. "And so it begins."

"Not funny, Luce. They're three—that's too young for relationship issues. Zach is going to have to deal with this tonight." Emma frowned and sat down next to Hannah. "Hey, Hannah. How's Clementine liking the childcare program?"

"I think it's safe to say she loves it. She gets up early every morning to get ready. The program challenges her and she talks nonstop about all her new friends."

"I'm so glad to hear that," Emma said. "The reports I've heard have been glowing. Clementine is very bright." She leaned closer. "Probably gifted, and she loves the interaction. The teachers adore her."

"Thanks for sharing that." Hannah smiled. "In truth, it makes it so much easier for me to leave her when I know she wants to be there."

"Of course. Trust me. It's hard for all of us." She met Hannah's gaze. "What do you think about your new boss?"

Hannah mulled the question for a moment, not sure how to answer.

Emma chuckled. "That wasn't a trick question."

"He's always prepared," Hannah finally said.

Once again, Emma laughed. "Isn't that, like, the Boy Scout motto?"

"I don't mean any offense," Hannah backpedaled.

"I'm very appreciative of the opportunity, but it's been a challenge to figure out Tripp."

"Yes. Welcome to our world," Emma said.

"How long have you and Lucy known him?"

"Eight years," Lucy piped in. "He was our first employee, followed by Dutch soon after. We started the ranch with six children and two heifers."

"Where is Tripp from?"

"Are you kidding? That drawl of his is pure Texoma." Lucy laughed. "Which reminds me, how's that horse challenge coming along?"

"Calamity Jane is very responsive. I have no doubts Tripp will win."

"Wonderful."

Emma glanced at her watch and then looked at her sister. "Who else is coming?"

"AJ was going to participate," Lucy said. "But she had an obstetrician appointment."

"Here I am," AJ called as she waddled into the room with a hand to her lower back. "I rescheduled."

"Was that wise?" Emma asked. "You look like you're ready to pop."

"I'm sure she means that in a good way," Lucy said.

"I'm fine," AJ said as she eased herself down to a bench. "I have two months left, and this baby is doing calisthenics already. They've checked me for gestational diabetes but everything is fine. Travis Junior is simply going to be a big kid."

"Football player," Lucy said.

"Yes. Naturally, Travis says OSU, but I'm pulling for crimson and cream. University of Oklahoma all the way."

Hannah listened to the friendly exchange, amused. She had only met AJ Maxwell, Travis's wife, once, but the spunky blonde ranch foreman was seven months pregnant and still out doing chores while driving the ranch all-terrain vehicle. She'd seen AJ's name on the schedule for fence checking just this week. Hannah would have to find a subtle way to bring that information into the next conversation with her stubborn boss. Though subtle probably wasn't going to work. The man needed a two-by-four wake-up call that she wasn't a fragile flower, nor a stick of dynamite ready to explode.

Lucy's gaze moved from Hannah's loose denim shirt to AJ's maternity top to Emma's baggy white oxford boyfriend shirt. She smiled and turned to Iris. "Okay, I don't know how this slipped past me. Could you check into staff maternity shirts?"

"I'm on it," the admin said as she scribbled on her clipboard once again.

"Good morning, ladies," Rue said as she strolled into the room with a travel mug of coffee in her hand. "What have you wrangled me into this time, Lucy?"

"Nothing dangerous. I promise," Lucy said.

"This from the woman who organizes scavenger hunts on the summer trail rides."

"This idea is much safer and there are no children involved. I'm trying to encourage more female members of the staff to get on board with the Pawhuska Orphanage outreach that the Timber Community Church does each year. Summer is our give back time. The guys took over the rodeo at the end of summer, but we need something targeted to involve women of all ages."

"What did you have in mind, Luce?" Emma asked. "It seems like we've done everything. I'm out of new ideas."

"Auctioning picnic baskets went well last year," Emma said.

"Then how about we auction off something even more intriguing. A bachelor, perhaps?" Rue suggested.

Lucy shook her head. "That leaves out our married women and we've had a spurt in those the last few years."

Rue eyed the women on the other side of the table over her mug. "True enough. I heard that sweet wrangler AJ hired, Josee Queen, is engaged."

"She is. He proposed just last night," AJ confirmed. "Marrying that nice vet, Trent Blaylock, thanks to our Hannah."

"Hannah? Are you a matchmaker?" Lucy asked with a smile.

Hannah's face warmed as all eyes turned to her. "No. The match has been in progress for months apparently. Trent asked, and I gave him a little advice on how to pop the question."

"It worked," Rue said. "Well played."

"What about you, Rue? Any plans to settle down?" AJ asked.

The doctor's eyes rounded. "I thought I was settled down. I'm retired after thirty years of being married to the army, aren't I?" She grinned. "Why would I want to complicate things?"

"I always sort of thought that you and Dutch might get hitched someday," AJ added with a conspiratorial wink.

Rue released an unladylike snort. "In the words of Dutch Stevens, if it ain't broke, don't fix it."

"You've never wanted to marry?" Emma asked.

Rue closed her eyes and opened them, glancing around the table. "I must be hallucinating. For a moment I thought we were at the Timber Big Hair Emporium slinging gossip like Aqua Net hairspray."

When AJ burst into a fit of giggles, Hannah put a hand to her mouth to suppress her own laughter. This was more fun than she'd had in a long time.

"Point well taken, Rue." Lucy held up a hand and chuckled. "Back to church business."

Emma wiped her eyes and took a deep breath. "What do you think about doing something along with the summer church picnic this year? The Sunday of Fourth of July weekend? Attendance is high with lots of tourists in town."

"Sounds like a great way to bring in donations for the orphanage," Rue said.

"We could do a fun run. Five kilometer," Lucy said.

"I'm sorry, but I do not run," Rue said. "At this stage in my life, trust me, if I'm running, I'm being chased."

AJ rolled her eyes. "I agree. Y'all can run if you like, but I cannot see myself even waddling five kilometers in this heat."

"How about an old-fashioned cakewalk?" Hannah asked. "Anyone with a spatula and a recipe can participate, and there's no real exercise involved."

All heads turned to her and she swallowed.

"Oh, my, this is a wonderful idea," Lucy said.

"How exactly does a cakewalk work?" Emma asked.

"We did them in my home church in Denver when I was growing up," Hannah said. "The cakes are on display before the event starts. Numbers are taped to the ground to form a circle. Tickets to participate are sold." She looked around to be sure everyone was following her explanation.

"Everyone who purchased a ticket starts walking on the numbered squares while the band plays music. When they stop playing music, you stop on a numbered square. A number is drawn from a hat and whoever is on that number gets to pick the cake of their choice and is out of the game."

"Does that mean some people don't get a cake?" AJ asked.

"Yes," Hannah said. "Usually there are consolation prizes offered."

"I like it!" Rue said. "We could do this in the church meeting hall. It would keep the cakes cool and we can easily tape numbers to the floor. In fact, I'm sure Dutch and some of his buddies will play music for us."

"Dutch plays an instrument?" Hannah asked.

"He plays a mean fiddle," Rue said. "His band will be playing at the Spring Social again this year."

"Spring Social?" Hannah asked.

"It's a town party with music and food, held the Friday night before the Fourth of July weekend celebrations," Rue said. "Long-standing tradition around here."

"Since the town of Timber is so supportive of Big Heart Ranch, we encourage staff support of the social, the rodeo and the parade," Lucy said. "So we hope to see you at as many events as you can get to."

"I see," Hannah said. Her stomach churned. She'd had a lifetime of being social.

Lucy turned to her administrative assistant. "Iris, what do you think about the idea? Will it bring in the younger women, as well?"

Iris nodded. "I like the cakewalk idea, but maybe it would add to the fun if the baker shares the dessert with the winner of their cake."

"But what if someone other than your fella picks your cake?" Emma asked. "You'd have to have dessert with them."

Lucy laughed. "Oh, the fun is in accidentally-on-purpose letting your fella find out which cake is yours. That obligates them to buy a ticket and play."

Rue burst out laughing. "Oh, Lucy, I like how you think. You're going to make quite a few menfolk squirm."

"And empty their wallets," Emma said.

"Occasionally, it's nice to have the upper hand," Lucy said with a serene smile.

"I'm in," Emma said. "Competition. Cake. What's not to like?"

"Oh, so am I," AJ said. "Hannah, this is a fabulous idea."

Hannah blinked as she realized what her idea had morphed into. Sharing her cake with someone? Suddenly her fabulous idea didn't seem quite so fabulous.

"We can have some fun prize drawings for those who enter their cake and ask the local businesses for contributions," Lucy added.

"I can handle that," AJ said. "It's hard to say no to an expectant woman, and I don't mind using my condition for the church."

"And I'm pretty good with graphic design," Iris said. "I can get some posters for the local businesses and see if the Timber Daily Gazette will give the church a discount in the Sunday paper."

"Great," Lucy said with a satisfied grin. "I'll notify Pastor Parr and I think the rest of the prep can be done by email."

"Isn't this all coming together nicely?" Emma said as she helped AJ to stand.

"It is," AJ added.

"I'm so glad you're on this committee, Hannah," Lucy said.

Hannah stared at her for a moment. Despite the fact that she'd disrupted their lives with her claims, the Maxwells treated her like she was one of them, with or without a DNA confirmation.

"Thank you, Lucy."

"Did I give you the number of the obstetrician in Pawhuska?" Lucy asked.

"Yes." Hannah grabbed her purse and stood. "I have an appointment scheduled."

"Great. AJ's baby shower is coming up. I hope you'll help us with that, as well. We'll have one for you and Emma in the fall," Lucy said.

"I'd be honored to help." She paused and glanced around. "But I don't even know if I'll be here in the fall."

Lucy looked up from her folder and got to her feet. "Why not? Clementine has started school. You have to settle somewhere. Why not Big Heart Ranch? You fit right in."

"I doubt that Big Heart Ranch will notice if I stay or leave," she said quietly as everyone else left the chow hall.

"Oh, that's not true. All of us will notice, especially Tripp."

"Tripp?" Hannah froze at the comment.

"Yes. I've seen the difference in him since you've been here."

Hannah stared at the eldest Maxwell, unsure of what to say.

"The man purposely avoids conversation." Lucy smiled. "It's like a game around here. Who can get the most words out of Tripp Walker? But lately, well, he's had a lot to say."

"I'm sure he does." Hannah grimaced. "My presence has irritated him from day one. For some reason, Tripp really doesn't like me much."

"Not true." Lucy shook her head as she, too, stood. "We have weekly staff meetings. You've been here two weeks, and he speaks highly of you."

"Really?"

"Yes. You know, Tripp is like all men who don't know how to express their feelings. They bark to protect us from finding out they're really a softie inside."

Hannah blinked. "I…I don't know what to say to that, Lucy."

"No response is required. Just keep in mind that maybe, just maybe, you're right where God wants you to be and the good Lord doesn't need any DNA test to tell you that."

"And here I thought things were going so well," Tripp said. He stomped into the stables with Dutch and Hannah following. "We've gone three weeks without any problems. Made it clear to another Friday, even."

"It's my fault, boss."

Tripp turned to Dutch, who now stood outside of the equine office. "Hannah is pregnant." He ground the words out. "You couldn't find anyone else to help you with the fences?"

"It isn't a terminal disease," Hannah murmured.

Dutch wiped his face with a red bandana and grimaced. When the old cowboy looked to Hannah, she stepped forward. Hands on hips, she shoved her dark waves off her shoulder and got right in Tripp's face. Fire lit her eyes as she met his gaze.

"Don't blame Dutch. It isn't his fault and I won't have him thrown under the bus for my actions. I told him it was okay for me to help and practically twisted his arm to let me assist."

Stunned, Tripp opened his mouth and closed it again. His quiet assistant had morphed into a raging spitfire.

"AJ is pregnant and so is Emma," Hannah continued. "They're still on the schedule. And for the record, I was simply helping. I rode in the ute."

He took a calming breath. "Your job is in the equine center. We've already had this discussion."

"I was all caught up in the office. Even the stable chores were completed."

"You can't play internet solitaire like everyone else?" he asked.

"You pay me for eight hours, so I work eight hours." She waved a hand at the office. "This is a bit under-challenging for my skill set."

"This is your job."

"I'm not going to collect my share of the winnings for doing nothing. That's not how I operate. If I don't earn the money, then I don't want the money."

Tripp shrugged. "I'm happy to take your share."

"That's not what I said. I intend to earn my share."

Dutch pulled off his straw cowboy hat and then slapped it back on as he looked from Hannah to Tripp. "Whoo-ee. You two are as much fun as being caught in a thunderstorm in your long johns." He turned on his heel.

"Where are you going?" Tripp asked.

"It's Friday afternoon. I'm a free man in two hours. I'm gonna go seek shelter until this particular storm passes."

Rue stepped into the stables as Dutch stomped out, her arms filled with a large crystal vase of flowers. Her gaze followed Dutch as she approached the office. "Everything all right in here?"

"Fine," Tripp said at the same time as Hannah.

"Sounds like it," she said. "These are for your assistant."

"Me?" A pleased smile curved Hannah's lips. She took the vase and brought it to her desk before plucking the card from the center.

"Lovely flowers, aren't they?" Rue said to Tripp.

Tripp glanced at the arrangement and scowled. He didn't know much about flowers, but they looked impressive and expensive. "Yeah. *Lovely.*"

"Trent Blaylock sent them."

"Trent? Why would the vet be sending Hannah flowers?"

Rue offered a secret little smile before she turned to leave. "Maybe you should ask her."

Tripp stared through the glass at Hannah, trying to figure out why the woman kept vexing him at every turn.

When his desk phone rang, Hannah picked it up. "Big Heart Ranch Equine Center. Hannah speaking." She nodded. "Sure. Let me ask Tripp."

She stepped out of the office with the portable phone in her hand. "Lucy wants to know if you can meet with her and the architect regarding the addition to the girls' ranch equine center on Monday."

"I thought you and Lucy were going to Tulsa for that lab testing Monday."

"She had to cancel," Hannah said.

Tripp resisted the urge to growl. Nothing was going right today, and now Lucy was messing with his calendar.

"What do you want me to tell Lucy?" Hannah asked quietly.

"Tell her I'm headed to the admin building now." He glanced at the flowers again. "Nice flowers."

"Thank you."

Tripp stomped to the administration building and straight past Iris Banner who manned the front desk, stuffing flyers into envelopes.

"Morning, Tripp."

"Morning." He kept moving down the hall, stopping in the doorway of Lucy's office. As always, he paused cautiously on the threshold before entering. Lucy's office had the distinction of looking like an Oklahoma twister just hit. It had gotten better since her husband hired Iris to help out. But not much.

"You can come in," she called from behind her desk.

He took a hesitant step into the dimly lit room. "I'm never sure if it's safe."

"It's before the F1 hits you have to worry. Not after."

"That's your story."

Lucy stood and stepped from around her desk. She cleared a stack of papers from a chair and gestured for him to sit.

"This is where you greet ranch guests?" Tripp asked.

"Give me some credit, Tripp. I use our very professional conference room for guests and business associates."

Tripp crossed his arms and frowned.

"We have established that you woke up on the wrong side of the bed." She sat down again and picked up a mug. "Will coffee help?"

"I'm good."

Lucy arched a brow as if to contradict that statement. "To what do I owe this pleasure?"

"Why did you cancel the DNA testing?"

"Is there a rush?"

"Hannah Vincent claims to be your half sister."

"That and two dollars will get you a pecan muffin at the Timber Diner. I don't understand the problem."

"What if she's not?"

She shrugged. "Then Hannah is an employee of Big Heart Ranch, like everyone else."

"Lucy, it seems to me you aren't taking this seriously. As I recall, you were pretty broken up the day she arrived."

"I was shocked. As was Hannah."

"What's changed?"

"I've had time to think and pray about the situation. Knee-jerking is never a good idea."

"I don't know. Going with my gut has served me well."

"What exactly is your gut telling you?"

He released a breath. "That maybe she's scamming the ranch."

"Tripp, I am the director of a children's ranch. Sixty children call Big Heart Ranch their forever home. Do you honestly think I wouldn't have Hannah checked out even more than the usual candidates?"

"So we're on the same page?"

"Not exactly. My page says cautious and yours says cynical and distrustful."

"Same thing."

"Not really. I've been where Hannah is. When I met Jack, you'll recall he was the in-house counsel for his aunt's foundation. The foundation that supports Big Heart Ranch. He thought we were snake oil salesmen."

Tripp nodded, recalling that day nearly two years ago.

"In addition to the regular background check, I've asked Jack to dig a little deeper."

"Slats Milburn says he found something."

Lucy's eyes rounded, and she shook her head. "Tell me you did not ask that slimy detective to snoop around in our business."

"I'm afraid I can't tell you that. What I can tell you is that I hired him and then fired him."

"You hired him, why? Because you thought I wasn't able to handle the situation?"

"When was the last time someone showed up at the ranch claiming to be your kin?"

This time Lucy groaned and rubbed the middle of her forehead with two fingers.

"I wasn't thinking," Tripp said. "We can agree on that. That's why I fired him before I even got a report."

"Then how do you know he has information?"

"He told me so, but I hung up on him."

"Maybe you better at least find out what the man has to say."

Tripp pushed his hat to the back of his head and grimaced. "I was afraid you'd say that."

"Please?"

"I'll do it." He met Lucy's gaze. "You don't believe she's Jake's daughter, do you?"

"It doesn't matter what I believe. What matters is that we are slow to judge and quick to love."

"Lucy, that doesn't answer my question."

The oldest Maxwell released a breath. "I've combed through those letters of Hannah's, and it's all about perspective. The way I see things, my father did have a relationship with Hannah's mother, but I believe they were very close friends. I don't read anything more than that into any of those missives. Hannah sees what she wants to see in those letters. Maybe what she needs to see."

"Are you going to tell her that?"

"I don't think that's necessary. Eventually, she's

going to figure that out for herself. When she does, it's our job to support her."

"You've obviously got something planned here."

"Actually, I don't. Hannah is a good person, and she's looking for what everyone at Big Heart Ranch is looking for. A second chance. Family. Unconditional love."

When Lucy met his gaze, he didn't like what he saw. "You got a second chance, Tripp. So did I. Does Hannah Vincent deserve anything less?"

"That's all fine and dandy, and it's plenty clear that you're a much nicer person than I am. But you have to tell her, eventually. Get the DNA testing done and all."

"I will. But can it hurt to put this off a little bit longer?"

"I don't know, Lucy. It might hurt more for her to go on thinking she's a Maxwell."

"I'd like Hannah to realize that she's safe here. Safe from whatever it is she's been running from." She looked him in the eye. "I think it's clear something has kept her off the grid and working far below her potential for the last few years."

Tripp was silent at the words. Lucy was right. Hannah had been on the run, with Clementine never leaving her sight.

"Look, Tripp, I'm giving Hannah the benefit of the doubt. But I'm also doing what's right for the ranch. I believe the good Lord sent her to Big Heart Ranch for a reason."

"A reason?"

"Maybe it's just that Hannah, Clementine and Hannah's unborn child need a family. This ranch is all about finding forever homes."

"I don't know," he grumbled.

"What have you got against Hannah Vincent?"

"Lucy, you believe in the good in everyone. I admire you for that. But I can't be that trusting."

"Why not, Tripp?"

Tripp rubbed the scar on his face. "I'm not going there. You're going to have to take my word on this." He looked away, shoving back memories of another single mother who was cavalier about her child and her pregnancy. "Trust has to be earned."

Chapter Six

Hannah opened the tailgate of the pickup truck and reached for one of the boxes of supplies stacked on the sidewalk outside the feed and tack store.

"Hold it right there, little momma," Dutch Stevens called out. He strode outside and stepped between her and the boxes. "You trying to get me in trouble with the boss?"

"This is becoming beyond ridiculous," Hannah muttered. "The West would not have been settled if homesteading women sat around doing nothing. Why, they had babies one day and were out baling hay the next."

"Yep."

"Ranch women are the unsung heroes of the West, in my opinion," Hannah continued. She was on a roll now and couldn't stop if she tried. All her frustration from the last few weeks bubbled over.

"You're preaching to the choir. Maybe you should take that up with Tripp."

Hannah groaned. "Take it up with Marshal Dillon? No, he doesn't listen to Miss Kitty. You should talk to him."

"Are you calling me Festus?"

"Dutch," she pleaded. "I need help."

The cowboy shook his head adamantly. "Hey, this ain't my circus. You may like living life dangerously, going toe-to-toe with the man, but not me. These are my golden years and I plan to cruise on autopilot straight to retirement. I am not looking for problems."

"Your golden years?"

"Yes, ma'am."

He chuckled as he lifted a box into the truck bed. "Pretty funny when you think about it."

"What's funny?"

"A little thing like you getting in Tripp's face on Friday. The man is at least six foot five."

"I'm glad I can entertain you." Hannah glanced down the street in time to see a tall, rail-thin cowboy get out of a rusty truck. The man narrowed his eyes and stared at her before he turned and started down the sidewalk toward the diner. "Dutch, who is that cowboy?"

"Slats Milburn."

"Who is Slats Milburn?"

Dutch heaved another box up and slid it into the bed of the pickup with a grunt. "Washed-up rodeo clown."

"What does a washed-up rodeo clown do for a living?"

"A little wrangling here and there. Odd jobs. Security. You know, watching herds and lots of such stuff."

"Such stuff?"

The wrangler leaned closer and did a quick look around. "Slats is the guy you call if you need to check something out," he said in hushed tones.

"Check something out?"

"You know, investigate your sister's new boyfriend, or locate your missing cattle. He's kind of sketchy, but he gets the job done. Slats is the guy who found AJ's horse when it was stolen. Though you didn't hear that from me."

"Seriously?" Hannah shivered as the man disappeared from sight.

"Somebody's gotta do it." Dutch dusted off his hands and wiped his forehead with his sleeve. He shot a quick glance at the sky before slamming the tailgate of the pickup shut. "Monday morning and it's already ninety degrees and nary a cloud in sight. Not a breeze to be found, neither. The only thing moving around here are the flies."

"Is it always this hot in mid-June?" Hannah asked.

"Depends on how fickle Mother Nature is feeling." He tossed his keys in the air. "Ready to go?"

Hannah nodded as Dutch stepped around the truck and plucked a flyer from the windshield before he got in the cab.

"What's this?" she asked, turning over the colorful paper on the seat between them.

"Timber Fourth of July rodeo is coming right up."

"Is anyone from Big Heart Ranch participating?" she asked Dutch.

"Oh, probably some of our young college-aged wranglers, but not the Maxwells. Travis had the good sense to retire after he nearly killed himself last year. And everyone else either has a bun in the oven or they're too busy with their own families and the ranch."

Dutch raised a palm to thank and acknowledge the truck behind him that waited as he backed out of the parking spot.

"What about Tripp?" Hannah asked.

"Oh, he never competes anymore. Used to, though, and he was good."

"Why not?"

"Tripp isn't about competition. Not an adrenaline junkie like most cowboys."

"He's doing the 100-Day Challenge," Hannah countered. "That's pretty competitive."

The cowboy turned left at the intersection of Main and Cedar Avenue and headed out of town. "That's just training them so they'll get adopted. Our Tripp is a bit of an animal activist. Lucy and Emma advocate for the children of Big Heart. Travis for the cows. AJ for the bison. And Rue looks out for those crazy chickens. Our Tripp advocates for every horse and donkey in a fifty-mile radius."

"How long has he been training horses?"

"No idea. Tripp Walker is a man of mystery. Showed up eight years ago when the ranch was getting started. Maybe you should ask him."

"Me?"

"He talks to you more than I've ever seen him talk to anyone outside of the Maxwells. While you're at it, could you ask him to share his prize-winning chili recipe? Been trying to get that for years."

"Tripp has a prize-winning chili recipe?"

"Yep, he's won every year since they started the competition at the ranch rodeo."

"Wait, there's a rodeo in Timber *and* at the ranch?"

"Missy, you're going to have to try to keep up." Dutch frowned, his bushy gray eyebrows nearly coming together.

"The Timber rodeo is part of the town's Fourth of July celebration. Mostly for the tourists. Our rodeo is for kids."

"Oh." She offered a nod.

Dutch looked at her and frowned. "No, you don't get it. This is huge. We have a full-on barbecue and chili cook-off with the rodeo. It's the end of summer for the kids visiting from the Pawhuska Orphanage, and all the children who graduated and left the ranch return. It's huge, I tell you. Huge. One of two times they open the ranch to the public. The other being Christmas."

"Wow. I had no idea." Hannah paused. "But you said Tripp isn't into competition."

"That's right. But he is into cooking. Whoo-ee can that man cook. He cooks and wins. No competition about it."

"Tripp cooks." She said the words with stunned disbelief.

"As I recall, AJ said the same thing. She found out what I'm talking about at Thanksgiving." Dutch laughed. "No one's ever mentioned this before?"

"That's a factoid I would not have forgotten."

"He's like some kind of gourmet. Why, the entire staff holds their breath at the holidays, waiting to find out what Tripp is going to bring. The man makes your taste buds roll over and beg for more."

Hannah blinked. "Tripp Walker?"

Dutch chuckled. "Sure enough. He has a big old cookbook held together by rubber bands and he has his own set of knives. Keeps them with his Bible. Man could easily have his own show on that cooking channel."

Hannah cocked her head and looked at him. "Are you pulling my leg?"

"Ask anyone. He's got these spinach lasagna roll-ups that melt in your mouth." A grin split Dutch's face. "It gets better. Tripp is a vegetarian."

"A vegetarian equine manager on a cattle and bison ranch who is a gourmet cook and wins the chili cook-off. Do I have that right?"

"Sure do." He smacked his lips. "Mmm, mmm. That's how good his chili is. Vegetarian chili and the man always wins." Dutch shot her a quick glance. "Wait a minute. You said you cook. Have you got a winning chili recipe in your back pocket?"

Hannah hesitated. "You know, I just might."

"Think about entering. There's a small cash prize, and they throw in some fancy pots and pans, oh, and dinner at the Oklahoma Rose."

"How small a cash prize?"

"I do believe it was one hundred dollars last year. But there's a fifty-dollar entry fee. The entry goes toward the orphanage in Pawhuska. They send the kids back at the end of summer with something for the facility. Last year it was a big-screen television."

Hannah pondered the idea for two seconds. "How do I sign up?"

"Iris over at the admin office will collect your money." Dutch laughed and slapped the steering wheel with his palm. "This is gonna be fun."

Hannah smiled serenely. She'd walked many roads in life and worn many hats, but the fact was she could cook. That was the reason the Dripping Falls Diner had called twice since she left, wanting to know when she was coming back.

If circumstances were different, she could work in any fine dining restaurant, but she chose to slide under the radar for Clementine. To protect her daughter.

"What kind of chili do you make?" Dutch asked.

"I can't tell you that." She turned back to the old cowboy. "Don't you tell him that I'm considering entering the contest."

"My lips are sealed. But if you're looking for someone to taste-test, I'm your man."

They rode in silence for moments. Finally, Dutch chuckled and shot her a glance. His eyes sparkled with mirth. "You sure you're up to this?"

"Excuse me? What's the big deal?"

"Tripp has an entire posse cheering him on."

"A posse?"

"Yep. People come out of the woodwork to watch him prepare his chili. They all pray for a sample before the judging."

Hannah stared at Dutch. "Tripp Walker?"

"Why do you keep asking me that?"

"I've been working with the man for nearly five weeks now and as far as I can tell, he's reclusive. I can't believe he'd be willing to be in the public eye."

"Tripp has a soft spot for orphans. He'll put up with a whole lot of attention if it will benefit orphans or horses. Maybe you should ask him about the stuff he does for the kids. Stuff he thinks no one knows about."

Hannah shook her head. "No. Haven't you heard anything I said? Tripp and I don't do well with conversation. I'm certainly not going to ask about his secrets."

"You two communicate. You just go at it like you're old married folk." He released a loud snort.

"That's not true at all," Hannah insisted.

"Sure it is. I think you like arguing with him."

Dutch approached the Big Heart Ranch security gate, rolled down his window and held out his electronic badge. When the arm slowly raised, he drove in and then turned left into the equine center parking area.

"I'm not about to let the man run over me," Hannah huffed. "And just because no one has ever dared to challenge him before doesn't mean I won't."

Laughter spilled from the wrangler as he turned off the engine and got out of the truck.

"What's so funny?" Hannah asked.

"Not a thing. Not a single thing." He grinned. "You know what, Hannah? You're all right. I hope you stick around."

"The Dutch seal of approval?" Hannah smiled at the cowboy, finding herself inordinately pleased with the words. Could it be she was really fitting in at Big Heart Ranch?

"You betcha." He nodded toward the truck bed. "Leave those boxes for now. I've got one of our college kids working with me for the summer. He's going to take care of them."

"What are you going to do next?"

"Got an appointment with Rowdy. I've been giving our resident troublemaker saddle time each day, getting him ready to be put in the schedule. Think I'll give him a little ride before the kids start showing up for lessons."

"I'm in the office if you need anything."

The sounds of a busy stable drifted into the open equine office as Hannah answered emails and checked inventory. Every now and then Dutch could be heard as he took long minutes grooming the gelding.

"Easy, boy," he murmured. "Don't you be pulling faces at me. I'm the boss here."

"Everything, okay, Dutch?" Hannah called.

"Aw, he's fine," Dutch called out. "We're friends, ain't we, Rowdy?"

When things got quiet, Hannah glanced at the clock. Nearly noon. Everyone was off grabbing lunch. The only sound was Dutch arguing with Rowdy.

An ominous chill raced over Hannah.

She got up and stood outside Rowdy's stall, debating whether she should say something. But the only words that came to mind were admonitions to use care. Dutch was an experienced horseman who wouldn't appreciate her interference any more than she would have appreciated his. Hannah bit her lip and kept her mouth shut.

The old cowboy eased the saddle on Rowdy and began to adjust the cinch. "Stand back. I can't say I trust this horse yet and the boss will cut off my mustache if he finds out it was my fault you got hurt."

"Hand me those grooming tools and I'll put them away," Hannah said.

When Dutch handed her a soft brush and currycomb, she headed to the tack room. A heartbeat later, Rowdy's agitated whinny filled the morning silence.

"What's got into you, boy?" Dutch said. "Whoa, Rowdy."

A loud bang echoed through the stables, followed by a reverberating thud.

"Dutch? Everything okay?"

Hannah raced back into the center aisle of the stables to Rowdy's stall. Dutch Stevens lay slumped against the wood slats. Panic slammed through her at the sight of his pale face, eyes closed. Her heartbeat pounded in her ears as she yelled his name. "Dutch!"

Ears flat, Rowdy ducked his head and shook his mane.

Without thinking, Hannah pulled open the stall door and stayed behind the gate, releasing Rowdy. The horse whinnied and danced, then burst out of the stall into the center arena of the stables, dragging his lead rope on the ground.

When the horse was clear, Hannah stepped into the stall. Kneeling in the hay, she slid her fingers to Dutch's neck and the carotid artery.

Her shaking fingers were rewarded with a pulse.

His breaths were shallow, though, and he remained unconscious.

A cursory check with her fingers revealed what seemed to be a small cut to the back of his head. Hannah grimaced at the amount of blood that covered her hand.

"Dutch, can you hear me?" She pulled her bandana from her pocket and applied pressure to the site while continuing to assess the cowboy.

"What can we do to help, Hannah?"

Hannah looked up at the voice, relieved to see Josee Queen and Tanya Starnes. Travis's lead wranglers leaned over the stall, their worried gazes moving from the agitated horse to the man on the ground.

"Call 9-1-1, and then get Rowdy into the corral. Keep the children out of here."

"Yes, ma'am," Tanya said with a nod.

"Whoa, boy. Easy," Josee murmured as she picked up Rowdy's lead rope.

Concerned staff rushed into the stables, offering assistance once Rowdy was outside.

Hannah kept her hand firmly on Dutch's wound as she yelled to another wrangler. "Someone please go and find Rue and Tripp."

Eyes fixed on the weathered cowboy, Hannah bit back tears and offered a silent prayer. *Take care of Dutch, Lord.*

The door to the bunkhouse creaked and opened. Hannah turned from her position leaning against the porch post. Rue Butterfield was silhouetted by the light of the kitchen.

"Is Clementine still sleeping?"

"Yes. Your daughter can sleep through anything."

"A blessing," Hannah murmured.

"Yes." Rue stepped onto the dark porch. "Honey, are you okay?"

Hannah nodded and gripped the railing. "I just can't stop thinking about Dutch." Every time she closed her eyes she saw the cowboy crumpled in the stall.

"The hospital tells me it's a few bruised ribs, a laceration to this head and a slight concussion."

"There was so much blood."

"Looked worse than it was. Those head wounds bleed heavily, so they stitched it up. Fortunately, that old cowboy has a hard head."

Hannah swallowed. "I've never been more scared."

"Yet, you responded like a pro. I'm so proud of you."

"Thank you, Rue." She frowned. "You're sure Dutch will be okay?"

"He'll be fine. I'd stay at the hospital but it might interfere with all the attention he's getting. Right now he's being waited on by a cute nurse who's doing neuro checks on him every hour and monitoring his IV antibiotics. Dutch is in cowboy paradise."

Hannah smiled.

"And trust me, he's going to milk this as best he can. It's not going to help that AJ will make him her special blackberry pie. Emma is no doubt right now whipping up chocolate muffins. Lucy can't cook so she'll go into Pawhuska for cookies from her favorite bakery."

"Dutch is well loved," Hannah murmured.

"Yes. That old codger is one of a kind." Rue offered a tender smile.

"What's Dutch's favorite cake?"

"Ha! You, too?"

"It'll be good practice for the cakewalk."

"All right then, German chocolate for sure." The older woman nodded as she settled into a rocking chair.

"He'll love that, though he'll likely not be able to get his swelled head through a door anytime soon."

"I can live with that," Hannah said. She turned to Rue. "Are you spending the night here?"

"If you don't mind?"

"Mind? No. Clementine and I love having you for a roommate."

"That's good because the summer has begun at Big Heart Ranch. Children from the orphanage are bussed in daily for vacation Bible study. The trail ride schedule is up and the ranch buddy plan is in full swing. I'm on call 24/7 from now until the end of August."

"I noticed how busy the stables have gotten."

"Busy is an understatement. But I wouldn't have it any other way."

Hannah glanced back inside the bunkhouse. "Would you mind keeping an ear out for Clementine? I'm going to take a walk."

"Sure. Take your time."

"Momma?" As if on cue, Clementine appeared at the door, her pink pony clutched under her arm. She rubbed her eyes with her fingers.

"I thought you were sleeping, sweetie," Hannah said.

"Can I have a glass of water?"

"May I?"

"May I?" Clementine repeated.

When Hannah stood, Rue put a hand on her arm. "Take your walk. I have this."

"You're sure?"

Rue nodded as she reached for the screen door. "It's a glass of water, dear. Go. We'll be fine."

Hannah strolled across the grass toward the gravel and dirt road. Ahead of her, the sun had dipped behind the old barn and now the only thing that remained was a soft pink glow against the velvety black sky. Reaching down, Hannah spotted a dandelion. She plucked the yellow flower and twirled it between her fingers.

With a low whistle, she called Jane and was rewarded by the soft thud of hooves pounding across the red dirt and hay as the horse moved across the pen in the dark. Hannah opened the barn door and turned on the switch that would illuminate the circular pen with a soft pink glow. Overhead, the mercury lamp sizzled.

From behind the fence, Jane offered Hannah a welcoming snuffle.

"Hey, girl, how you doing tonight?"

The horse nodded her head in response and nudged her nose through the fence in greeting. Hannah rubbed the mare's satin neck and stared deep into her dark chocolate eyes.

"You're going to win, Jane."

Jane nickered.

"Are you ready to practice?" Without waiting for a response, Hannah walked around the outside of the fence in a complete circle with Jane following on the inside.

Hannah stopped.

Jane stopped.

Hannah changed direction and the horse did the same.

"Good girl. Now let's walk backward." Hannah stepped back and so did Jane."

They repeated the process over and over again until Hannah stopped to reward Jane with a nose rub.

"Good girl."

"What are you doing?"

Hannah tensed and whirled around to face Tripp. "A

little protected contact training. You'll note that I am not in the pen."

"So I see." He glanced at Jane. "You two have done this before."

"A time or two."

"I knew something was going on. Never have seen a horse so willing to follow."

"She's an amazing horse." Hannah turned to Jane and smiled.

"You're falling in love with this mare," Tripp said after a minute.

"Maybe," Hannah murmured, turning back to Jane.

"Not a good idea, Hannah. She's going to auction after the challenge."

"It can't hurt anything to love her."

"As long as you can let go," he said softly. He, too, turned to Jane. "She sure likes getting attention from both of us."

"Hasn't hurt anything. I think it only ensures she's going to be a winner." Hannah smiled. "Besides, I'm not really training her. Just following up on what you've already done."

"Don't sell yourself short. I was watching for quite a while."

Hannah smiled to herself.

"Have you been inside the pen?"

She glanced at him. "I promised I wouldn't."

Tripp seemed to relax at her words. He stood next to Hannah, loped his arms over a rail of the fence and stared out into the night. Before them the sky stretched far and wide, unobscured by buildings. A thin band of crimson from the departing sunset continued to back-light the darkness.

"Red sky," Tripp observed.

"You can almost smell the rain coming in. The air is heavy with loam," Hannah agreed.

"We could use a good storm, though Travis won't be too happy."

"Travis?"

"AJ and Emma are out of commission for trail rides this year. So he's replacing them. Three days under the stars with the ranch children. Rain can make things mighty uncomfortable."

An easy silence stretched between them as they stood enjoying the evening. The sound of frogs and crickets could be heard from the pond. A barn owl hooted in the distance.

"You saved Dutch's life today," Tripp said.

"I did exactly what you would have done."

"Maybe so. But you didn't panic. You were calm. Directed the staff and kept the children out of the way." He shook his head.

She shrugged. "Like I said. You would have reacted exactly the same."

"Still, pretty impressive."

"For a pregnant woman?" she asked quietly.

"Touché," he returned.

"What will happen to Rowdy?"

"I suspect our Rowdy is claustrophobic. The trailer episode and now in the stall. I'll start by grooming him outside to help his stress and break his response patterns."

"You'll have time to work with Rowdy and train Jane?"

Tripp gestured with a hand. "This is my life."

"I'll do what I can to help more."

"Help more? Is that possible?"

"I can muck stalls. I asked my doctor. He said no

riding, of course, but anything that I'm used to doing I can do. With reasonable caution."

Tripp eyed her. "You mucked stalls in Mudville?"

"*Dripping Falls*. And no, but I scrubbed the kitchen on my hands and knees." She met his gaze. "I'll be careful."

"We can talk about it."

Hannah exhaled. *We can talk about it* translated to *topic dismissed*. Would he dismiss her if she was a Maxwell? "Lucy and I go to Tulsa for the DNA testing on Wednesday," she said.

He nodded but said nothing.

"We should have the results in forty-eight hours."

Once again, he didn't respond but continued to keep his attention focused on the mare who moved gracefully around the pen.

"Listen, I want to apologize," Tripp murmured.

"For what?" she asked.

"Come on, you know for what."

"There are so many things. You're going to have to be specific."

A tenuous smile touched his lips. "I've been a bit harsh."

"Yes. You have been. Why is that?"

"I'd say I jumped to conclusions."

"That's *what*. I asked why."

"Hard to explain."

"I've got all night."

"Yeah," he said with a nod. "It might take that long."

She stared at his profile in the soft light. His strong nose and firm lips. Once again, she was impressed by how the scar running down his face only added to his character.

"What happened to your face?" Hannah dared to ask, surprised at her own boldness.

Tripp swallowed and blinked slowly. "My mother pushed me through a window."

Hannah worked hard not to gasp. "How old were you?"

"Sixteen. She was so strung out, she didn't know what she was doing."

"But your mother?" Hannah could barely say the words. "Where is she?"

"She died giving birth. A drug baby. Didn't make it past his first few days." The words were void of emotion.

"I'm so sorry."

"I'm not asking for pity, Hannah."

"Good thing I wasn't offering any." She took a deep breath as she tried to make sense of his tragic admission.

The urge to reach out and touch Tripp Walker was strong. Unable to resist, Hannah reached up and gently touched the scarred side of his face.

Tripp stiffened. Then he covered her hand with his and turned to face her. In that moment, something flickered in his eyes and his gaze almost became tender. Hannah's chest tightened, and she nearly forgot how to breathe.

Then he released her hand and stepped away, his gaze returning to the mare.

"Mothers are supposed to protect their children," Hannah said, her voice shaky.

"Doesn't always work like that." He nodded toward the brick houses in the distance. Home to the children of Big Heart Ranch. "That's what this place is all about."

Hannah nodded.

"You've been protecting Clementine. Hiding out," he said. Not a question, but a statement.

"Yes." Hannah released a sigh. She was so weary of the sad story of her life.

Tripp faced her again and leaned close. Close enough that she could see the dark circle around the amazing blue of his eyes and smell the scent of horse, hay and man. His gaze skimmed her face as though searching for something. Then he stuffed his hands in his pockets.

"It's getting late," he murmured.

"Yes. It is."

"Good night, Hannah."

"Good night, Tripp."

The cowboy walked away, leaving Hannah trying to figure out what just happened. They'd passed some sort of milestone in their relationship, but she didn't know if she should be pleased or terrified.

Hannah turned to Jane. The wild mustang was much easier to figure out.

Chapter Seven

Something was off. Hannah felt it in the air when she got up in the morning and struggled into her jeans. She was entering her second trimester, and it was about time to break out the maternity clothes that announced to the world that she was a single and pregnant mother.

The good news was she could eat bacon again. Morning sickness had passed.

An envelope addressed to Hannah in Rue's handwriting was propped on the kitchen counter next to the empty cake plate that had held a German chocolate cake a week ago. She slid the notepaper from the envelope.

"Dutch ate the entire cake and says thank you. He also says if your chili is as good as your cake you're going to give Tripp a run for the prize money."

So much for keeping her entering the chili cook-off a secret. Hannah smiled. The old cowboy was supposed to be back at work next week. She missed one of her favorite curmudgeons.

The week had been strange enough as it was without Dutch. Tripp seemed to be avoiding her since their late-night conversation at Jane's corral. Fine, the horse whisperer didn't do well with people. There was no doubt that she had terrified the man. If only he knew that he scared her, too.

Hannah couldn't explain her behavior that night. It was unlike her and she had no defense, except that unless she was arguing with the man, being around Tripp made her all fluttery and nervous at the same time. Arguing was safer, because the rest of the time, she longed to take away the sadness in his eyes. Saving Tripp Walker wasn't her place. She had enough of her own issues to deal with.

"Ready, Clemmie?" Hannah asked her daughter.

"We're early, Momma. The clock hands aren't where they're supposed to be."

"Clementine, sometimes we have to change our routine and that's okay. Momma has a lot of work to do today because it's Friday and the end of the month."

"Friday means that it's almost time for pancake Sunday again. Right?" Clementine said. She hopped from her seat and carried her empty oatmeal bowl to the sink.

Hannah rinsed the bowl and placed it in the dishwasher.

"Right, Momma?"

"Right," Hannah said.

As she answered, she suddenly realized what today was, besides Friday. *Today is the day.*

Hannah glanced at the calendar and shivered. It had been forty-eight hours since she and Lucy had gone to Tulsa for the DNA lab work.

"Where's Miss Rue?" Clementine asked.

"She's out on a trail ride. She'll be back tonight."

"I miss her," Clementine said.

"Me, too. Now go brush your teeth and I'll grab your backpack."

"Yes, Momma."

Hannah picked up the pink backpack from the foot of Clementine's bed. She carefully tidied the quilt and smoothed her daughter's pillow. Glancing around, she noted all the little touches that served to make the bunkhouse feel like home.

Clementine's drawings were tacked to the bulletin board. A bouquet of black-eyed Susan mixed with daisy fleabane picked in the ranch pasture sat on the table between her bed and Clementine's. Propped on Clementine's bureau was a paper menu from the Timber Diner that the five-year-old liked to peruse on Saturday nights before she went to bed, even though she always ordered strawberry pancakes.

Was this their forever home or only another stop on the way? Hannah couldn't shake the ominous feeling that crowded her, dogging her steps as she locked the bunkhouse door and walked to the childcare building while holding her daughter's hand. Once she dropped Clementine off, she started in the direction of the equine center.

The air was thick with the humidity. Low clouds had lingered all week, trapping the world in a dismal gray blanket with either a threat or a promise of rain, depending on your perspective. Hannah preferred sunshine to this gloom.

The light was on in the equine building and the repetitive sound of shovels mucking stalls could be heard as she walked to the office. Nose buried in his laptop, Tripp didn't even look up when she walked in.

"Lucy wants to meet with you at the admin building around nine if that works for you."

Good morning to you, too, Tripp.

"Okay," she said.

Hannah kept her eye on the clock as she worked

through the monthly ordering. "I'm ready to send out the feed order for July," she said. "Anything special you wanted to add before I hit Send?"

"No. I'm good."

The only sound in the office was the loud tick of the second hand on the industrial wall clock. It was five minutes to nine. Hannah turned off the monitor. At the last minute, she grabbed her purse from the desk drawer. Just in case.

"I guess I'll get going," she murmured.

Tripp merely nodded.

Hannah counted her steps as she walked along the sidewalk to the administration building.

"Fifty-seven."

Why was she nervous? Jake Maxwell had to be her father. What other explanation could there be for the letters to her mother?

"Ninety-six."

What if he's not? What then?

She stood outside the admin building, staring at the double glass doors.

Then I'll start over. I know how to start over.

Hannah opened the door and stepped inside. Her boots echoed on the tile floor as she walked up to the reception desk. Iris met her gaze.

Was that pity in her eyes?

"Good morning, Hannah." Lucy's admin put a smile on her face. "Is it still dreary out there?"

"Uh, yes, still gray."

"We certainly could use the rain," Iris continued.

"Rain," Hannah murmured, trying to focus. She glanced up at the clock. "I have a nine o'clock appointment with Lucy."

"Yes. Of course. Head on back to the conference room. She's expecting you."

When she entered, Lucy greeted her with a smile. "Hannah." Emma was also in the room. Both stood when she entered and both wore awkward smiles on their faces.

"I hope you don't mind that baby Daniel is here." Lucy waved a hand toward the portable play yard in the back of the room.

"No. Of course not."

Lucy picked up the landline on the table. "Iris, hold all our calls. I'd like no interruptions."

Hannah swallowed back the dread. "DNA results?"

Emma glanced at Lucy, who nodded and shuffled through the files in front of her. "Hannah, I've given this a lot of thought and prayer. I believe our father was a very close friend to your mother. Unfortunately, we, like you, have very few physical memories." She paused and met Hannah's gaze.

Hannah heard everything in Lucy's pained expression and bowed her head before the words reached her ears.

"The results are back on the DNA test. They show no match."

No match.

No family. No plan. No resources.

Nothing.

Nausea choked Hannah. Her heart pounded against her temples and for a moment darkness swallowed her. She gripped the chair arms, willing herself not to pass out. "I should leave."

"Leave?"

She reached for her purse. "Leave Big Heart Ranch. I'm so embarrassed."

"There's nothing to be embarrassed about," Emma said. Anguish laced her words. "I think we can conclude that your mother and my father must have been very close friends who communicated during a difficult time in her life."

"And I jumped to conclusions because I needed to believe…" Hannah couldn't say the words aloud. *I needed to believe that I was connected to someone. That I had a family. That I mattered to someone.*

"That's not what I'm saying," Emma said. "Jake and Anne's friendship brought you to Big Heart Ranch. You have to believe that you're here for a reason. I do."

"Exactly," Lucy said. "Please, Hannah, we're here for you." Lucy reached out to touch her hand. "We don't want you to leave."

Hannah swallowed. "I need to think."

"Sure. Absolutely," Lucy said. "Take the rest of the day off if you need to."

Clementine. She had to find her daughter.

The sky opened up as she walked back to the childcare building. Rain soaked her, drowning her tears.

"Here, take this umbrella for Clementine," her daughter's teacher said.

Hannah carried Clementine to the Honda parked behind the bunkhouse before she dashed into the cottage to collect a change of clothes for her and Clementine. She opened her bureau and shoved her hand to the back and pulled out an envelope filled with crisp bills. All her paychecks from the ranch that she had cashed and squirreled away for the future. A future she was unsure of, but a future far from this particular moment in time.

Hannah looked at the scribbled tally on the outside of the envelope.

It wouldn't get them far. Back to Missouri and then

they'd have to find another furnished apartment and a reliable vehicle.

Maybe she should have taken the offer from her grandmother's estate. Then she wouldn't have to have a backup plan.

No. That money came with too many strings. She could never do that to Clementine or her baby.

"But Momma. Today is watercolor paint day," Clementine said when Hannah returned to the Honda and checked the straps on the booster seat.

"I'll buy you some paints today. Let's take a ride and get ice cream for lunch and pancakes for dinner." She just needed a little time to think and plan. Everything would be fine. It was always fine once she had a plan.

The little car made a funny noise before the engine finally turned over. Hannah released a breath. The windshield wipers slapped an even rhythm as the rain beat down on the windows.

Miles down the road, on the outskirts of Timber, the car began to sputter. Hannah revved the engine. That helped for a moment, but relief was short-lived when minutes later the Honda coughed and choked in earnest.

"Don't die on me now, baby," she muttered as she pulled the vehicle off the road. Another shudder and the vehicle gasped its last breath.

Hannah slapped her palm against the steering wheel of the Honda.

"Momma, is everything okay?"

"Just fine, sweetie." She fumbled in her purse for the ranch cell phone Tripp insisted that she keep with her at all times.

No. She wasn't going to call Tripp. She could handle this. She'd handled the last seven years without Tripp

Walker saving her. Hannah nearly laughed out loud at the idea of Tripp being her knight in shining armor.

The man would give her a lecture about being an irresponsible mother before he'd do any saving.

"Momma, I'm hungry."

Hannah checked the time on the phone. "I guess you usually get a morning snack around now at school."

"Uh-huh."

"Let me see what I have in my bag." Hannah foraged around the tote bag she'd grabbed and pulled out a box of animal crackers. "Will this do?"

"Oh, yes, please." Clementine reached forward and took the box. "My favorite. Thank you."

While Clementine ate and drew pictures in the condensation in the back seat window, Hannah took out her worn Bible. She flipped the pages, reading underlined verses.

"Momma, what are you doing?"

"Preserving my sanity." She knew only too well that her daughter was going to ask another dozen questions before something else distracted her.

"Momma, are you talking to yourself?"

Hannah raised her head from the pages. "I'm talking to God, Clemmie."

"What's He saying?"

"Right now I'm doing all the talking."

"My teacher says you have to be silent sometimes so you can hear God."

She released a long sigh and couldn't help but smile at the words. "That's right."

Wiping the fog from her window, she peeked outside. The rain had stopped while they sat in the vehicle. Hannah rolled down the window a few inches and let the cleansing breeze, ripe with the sweet fragrance of grass and plants, fill the car.

"Are we going to stay here all day?" Clemmie asked.

"No. We are definitely not going to stay here all day." Hannah met her daughter's expectant gaze in the rearview mirror. The five-year-old's expression clearly asked, *What's the plan?*

"See if you can find a camel in that box, okay?"

Hannah closed her own eyes for a moment. When she opened them, a flash of red and blue lights in the rearview mirror caught her attention. Hannah turned around to see a Timber police vehicle approaching. Her stomach did a complete drop to the floor.

"Are we in trouble?" Clementine pushed her springy curls away from her face and turned around in her booster seat.

"No, sweetie. The nice policeman is here to help us." *Because this day can't possibly get any better,* she silently added.

The officer got out of his vehicle and approached. A middle-aged man with salt-and-pepper hair, he wore a gray Stetson with his dark gray uniform.

"Ma'am, is there a problem?"

"My vehicle died."

"I'll call the Timber Garage. In the meantime, may I see your license and registration?"

"Certainly, officer." Hannah rummaged in her purse and handed over the paperwork and her license.

He glanced from her license to her. "Missouri?"

"I'm temporarily staying at Big Heart Ranch."

"That so? Haven't had the pleasure." He offered a hand. "I'm Chief Daniels."

"Hannah Vincent and—"

"I'm Clementine," her daughter piped in.

"Pleased to meet you." The man grinned as he peeked into the back seat to look at Clemmie. "I've got a few grandchildren about her age." He nodded toward his cruiser. "It'll take a moment to run this information."

A few minutes later Chief Daniels approached the Honda again. "Ma'am, I'm going to need you to step out of the vehicle."

Hannah swallowed as adrenaline shot her heart rate into overdrive. "My daughter, too?"

"No, ma'am. Your daughter can stay in the car while you and I chat."

She opened the door and stepped outside. "Ma'am, I need you to keep your hands where I can see them."

"Yes, sir." Hannah folded her hands as if in prayer.

"Are you aware this vehicle is stolen?"

"What?"

"Plates and VIN match up to a vehicle stolen from Oklahoma City six months ago."

"I have a bill of sale from a used car dealer in Denver."

"Do you have that paper with you?"

"Yes. Of course. I have all the paperwork the dealer gave me." A fat drop of rain plopped onto her face. Hannah brushed it away with the back of her hand.

Chief Daniels glanced up at the sky where dark clouds had gathered. "Tell you what. I'm going to take you down to the station and we'll sort it all out in the comfort of our brand-new climate-controlled building in downtown Timber."

"Is that necessary? I told you I work at Big Heart Ranch."

"Just until all this is straightened out." Chief Daniels opened Clementine's door.

"Momma, are we going to ride in the police car?"

"Yes, Clementine. Our car is broken so the nice police chief is going to give us a ride."

"Yippee," Clementine said as she unfastened her booster seat and leaped into her mother's arms.

"This wasn't the plan I hoped for, Lord," Hannah said under her breath as she scooped up Clemmie.

Overhead, thunder cracked and a streak of light shot across the sky like a bottle rocket.

"Fine," she muttered, closing her mouth.

"Seriously, Chief? You arrested a single mother and a five-year-old?"

"Now calm down, Tripp. I didn't exactly arrest them. Took her statement and Ms. Vincent asked me to call you."

Tripp glanced around the stainless steel and tile office. "Where are they?"

"They're in the interrogation room. I gave the little girl milk and cookies and her momma is reading back issues of *Cowboy* magazine."

"Why are you holding her?"

"She's driving a stolen vehicle. Well, not exactly driving. That thing is held together with two rubber bands and a paper clip. We towed it to our impound lot." Chief Daniels frowned. "I'll have to check on the protocol, but you know, with a child involved in this situation, I may need to call social services."

Tripp winced, his gut taking a hit at the words. *Not Clementine.* No way was that going to happen.

"Is that necessary? Hannah is my assistant at the ranch."

"She is?"

"Fact is we're friends. Closer than friends."

Chief Daniels blinked and his eyes popped. "You are?"

"Yes, sir. We're, uh… She and I are…" He took off his cowboy hat, slapped it back on and cleared his throat as he worked desperately to find a way around the situation without digging himself any deeper. "Close," Tripp repeated.

A grin of pure surprise split the chief's face. "Well, I'll be. Why didn't you say so? Wait until I tell the missus." Chief Daniels shook his head again. "Sure are closemouthed about your personal life. I suppose we can dispense with calling social services under the circumstances."

Relief ripped through Tripp. "Thank you. Hannah and Clementine live at Big Heart Ranch."

"I can remand her to your custody then while I turn the vehicle over to the Denver Police. I've taken a full report. She claims she paid cash for the vehicle right before she drove out here." He met Tripp's gaze. "That true?"

"Doesn't she have a bill of sale?"

"Yeah, but I called over to Denver. Can't find any trace of the dealer. They admit he could have been there, but the lot is empty. Nothing but cement and an empty building."

"Hannah arrived in late May. Been at the ranch all this time. Lucy hired her and did a complete background check."

"That makes two of us. She's clean. Not even a traffic ticket." Chief Daniels scratched his head. "Though I should ticket her for not getting the car registered. She's been here six weeks."

"The car wasn't worth registering."

"Just the same."

"Come on, Chief. Cut her some slack. Hannah drove

here straight from her grandmother's funeral in Colorado with a tank of gas, her little girl, and not much more than that."

"Fine. Fine. This is an election year. And I guess I do owe Big Heart Ranch a few favors for making me look good by breaking up that horse thieving ring last year." He smiled. "And Mrs. Daniels does like happy endings. Can't wait to give her a call."

Tripp squirmed at the words. "So can she go?"

"Sure, don't have to tell you she shouldn't leave town, in case the Denver Police have questions. For now, we'll consider this poor judgment." He clucked his tongue. "Shame she's out what she paid for the vehicle. But at least she's not in jail. Next time you might consider helping your little woman with her vehicle purchasing decisions."

Tripp nearly choked. *Little woman.* Hannah would have something to say about that term.

"How soon until you can release her?" Tripp asked.

"Now works for me." Chief Daniels walked down to a small room with a two-way window on the outside. He opened the door. "Ms. Vincent, your... Tripp Walker is here."

Hannah jumped up, her gaze shifting to him with relief. If only she looked that glad to see him all the time.

"Mr. Tripp," Clementine cried. "We got to ride in a police car with the lights and sirens."

Tripp ran a hand over his face. "Really, Chief?" he muttered.

"The little girl asked for all the bells and whistles. I was happy to oblige."

"Are we leaving?" Clementine asked, her gaze going from Tripp to Chief Daniels.

The chief nodded as he handed Hannah a sheaf of

paperwork. "Sorry for the inconvenience, ma'am. Here's a copy of your paperwork, just in case."

When they stepped into the central area of the station, Hannah glanced at the stack of her belongings on the station floor, along with Clementine's booster seat. "Thank you for getting my stuff from the Honda, Chief Daniels."

She reached for a box, but Tripp intercepted and grabbed everything in two hands.

"Clementine, can you take your backpack?" he asked the little girl.

"Yes, Mr. Tripp." Clementine smiled as she followed him through the double doors and out of the police station. "They have the best cookies there," she said with one last glance through the glass.

Hannah settled Clementine into the back seat of the truck while Tripp placed her belongings in the flatbed.

"Well, that was fun," Hannah said as she stepped up on the running board and into the pickup.

Tripp fastened his seat belt and turned to her. "Hannah, I don't think you understand the implications of what just happened."

Hannah stared at him like he was a two-headed cow. "Excuse me?" She glanced in the back seat and lowered her voice. "I was there. I understand completely. And it hasn't escaped me that I was ripped off a thousand dollars by a con man and arrested for my troubles."

"You weren't arrested." Tripp shook his head. "Be grateful for that. Employees have been terminated at Big Heart Ranch for less."

"Are you telling me I'm going to be fired?"

"It's possible. If anyone gets wind of this."

"I happen to have an impeccable job record up to

now." Panic flashed through her eyes. "And he didn't officially arrest me."

"That's because he thinks you and I are..." Tripp swallowed. "He thinks we're..."

Hannah's eyes rounded. "You told him I'm your what?"

"I didn't exactly tell him anything. I just didn't correct his assumptions."

Hannah groaned and rubbed her forehead, pushing her hair off her shoulders.

"Look, I can think of a lot worse things than having Chief Daniels assume that—"

"Oh, really?" Hannah asked. "Neither of us can even say the words out loud. That's how horrified we both are by those assumptions."

"*Horrified* is kind of harsh. I'm a little embarrassed."

"I embarrass you?"

"No. I didn't say that."

"Sure you did." Hannah shook her head. "But it hardly matters. Having people think I'm... That you and I are..." She stumbled over her words. "All I can tell you is that I'm used to people sneering first and asking questions later. Being a single mother seems to be a free-for-all for everyone to voice their opinions and judge me. And they do."

"I think it's possible you're exaggerating. Besides, no one is judging you at Big Heart Ranch."

"Right. Like you never judged me."

He opened his mouth and closed it again, not willing to risk a lightning strike for denying her charge.

"You probably ought to know that the chief had been considering calling social services."

Hannah gasped. "You probably should have told me that right away." Her dark eyes pleaded with him. "Why would he do that?"

"Just doing his job. I told him it wasn't necessary, and he agreed when I alluded to…"

"Yes. I get it."

"Chances are that's the end of the whole thing," Tripp said, hoping he sounded upbeat.

"That's not how it works in my world," Hannah muttered.

They drove in silence for several miles before Tripp checked his rearview mirror. Clementine had fallen asleep. The little girl's pumpkin-colored tresses were a wild and frizzy disarray from the weather. His heart melted.

He had never considered the possibility of having a family, but today, something changed and he realized that having the chief think he and Hannah were… Well, it wasn't the end of the world.

"Where were you going when the Honda broke down?" he asked.

"I was going to fill up with gas and head back to Dripping Falls. They're holding my job for me."

"Why?"

"You know why. You knew before I went to see Lucy, didn't you?"

"So when the going gets tough, Hannah Vincent packs her bags," Tripp said.

"That is not true. I move to keep Clementine safe."

"She's safe here."

"Tripp, I've made a fool of myself."

"Only a handful of people know why you came to Big Heart Ranch, and they're the people who care about you. Truth is, everyone likes you and Clementine."

"I don't know about that," she murmured.

"I do."

Tripp turned to Hannah and saw the battle going on in her head reflected on her face.

"So your plan is to pluck Clementine from her friends at Big Heart and take her back to Mudville without looking back?"

"Dripping Falls."

"Whatever."

Once again, she massaged her forehead. "I generally have a plan. This time everything caught me by surprise."

"What about Calamity Jane? You're on the challenge agreement as assistant trainer."

She released a bitter laugh. "Assistant trainer of a horse I don't get to train."

"Be that as it may, you agreed."

Hannah was silent.

"I don't want to pull out the paperwork, but you and I had an agreement. I can't train Jane without your help, and you have a legal responsibility to help me."

"I never signed any legal documents."

"We shook on it. A gentleman's good faith agreement. That's legal around these parts. They used to hang a man for breaking an agreement."

"Why am I not surprised? This is the most convoluted state I have ever stepped foot in."

He continued, ignoring her rant. The more he talked, the more important keeping Hannah at Big Heart Ranch seemed and he wasn't quite sure why.

"Lucy has an ugly mustard-colored Honda she holds on to for sentiment. I'll have Dutch take it in for an oil change and you can drive it."

Hannah shot up in the seat, outrage splashed all over her face. "No. Absolutely not." When Clementine stirred in the back seat, she lowered her voice again. "I don't need handouts or charity. I can do it myself or I can do without."

Tripp shrugged. "Life is all about handouts. One way or another, you can't always do it all yourself."

"Sure, I can."

"You're missing the point. The hard part is learning to play on the team. Clementine deserves that."

"You do it all yourself. You don't need anyone." She slid him a pointed glance. "I'd hardly call Tripp Walker a team player."

He grimaced at her words. Trust Hannah to find the buttons to push. "Maybe we both need a lesson in team sports."

"Maybe."

Hannah turned to the window. Her chocolate-brown hair was all wavy and full from the rain and provided a curtain between them, hiding her face and her emotions.

"You okay?" he asked.

"I was so sure that Jake Maxwell…" She took a deep breath. "I'm weary. It's battle after battle and I'm always taking two steps forward and one step back. I'm just tired, Tripp."

Tripp longed to pull the car over, take her in his arms and tell her it would be all right. But Hannah would be the first to tell him that *all right* was a fairy tale, and he hadn't believed in fairy tales in a long time, either.

"I told you. You don't have to do it all alone. Let your friends help you."

"I'm not used to having friends."

"Yeah. I get that. But you've been here six weeks now. It's time you accept the fact that we like having you around."

She turned in her seat and searched his face. "Are we friends?" The words were barely a whisper.

"Yeah, we are."

As Tripp stared into her sad eyes, he realized he

didn't want Hannah and Clementine to leave. He swallowed hard at the revelation, shoving it to the back of his mind to examine at another time.

Tripp dropped Hannah and Clementine off at the bunkhouse and brought her box of stuff from the Honda inside for her.

When he turned to leave, Clementine put her hand in his and tugged. "Mr. Tripp, how will we get to the parade next week if our car is gone?"

He knelt down next to her and gently tugged an orange corkscrew curl. "No worries, little pumpkin. I'm taking you."

Clementine threw her arms around his neck. "Oh, thank you, Mr. Tripp, for saving us."

Tripp didn't dare look up and meet Hannah's gaze. He knew what she thought about Clementine's admission. Instead, he stepped out the back door and pulled out his phone as he headed back to the pickup.

"Slats, this is Tripp Walker. I want to know what you found on Hannah Vincent."

"That's going to cost."

Tripp grit his teeth. He knew what was coming. "I already paid you."

"That was weeks ago. The price of information is fluid, and it so happens that it just went up." The cowboy chuckled. "I'll need twice what you paid me."

"Fine. I'll look for you at the Timber Rodeo."

"Sorry, I've got bigger fish to fry. I'll let you know when I'm back in town."

Tripp disconnected the call. Slats was going to gouge him good. Didn't matter. He needed to know if there were any more surprises before Hannah got herself into any more trouble.

Chapter Eight

"No, thank you." Hannah opened a kitchen drawer and searched through the papers. She pulled out the drawer itself, just in case something had fallen behind. "I think the Spring Social is a fine idea. You two go and have fun. I'm not interested."

"Now, Hannah, don't you want to hear me play the fiddle?" Dutch asked.

"Hmm?" She turned and met Dutch's gaze. The bow-legged wrangler was all spruced up in a starched white Western shirt with pearl buttons. He wore a silver trophy buckle with his black Levi's.

Hannah smiled and reached out to straighten his black-and-turquoise bolo necktie. "You look so handsome."

The cowboy blushed bright crimson and shook his head. "There's no talking sense to her. I'm gonna wait in the truck."

Hannah glanced around the room and then stepped to the other side of the kitchen to inspect the small stack of cookbooks that she had brought along from Missouri. She carefully flipped through the pages of each book.

"Emma and Lucy have a babysitter who is happy to watch Clementine, too," Rue said. "You have plenty of time to get ready. It doesn't start until dusk. Dutch and I are going early so I can help him set up. His ribs are still sore."

"Poor Dutch." Hannah raised her head. Rue also wore a white Western shirt, hers paired with a long denim skirt and square-toed brown boots with a wing design. Silver and turquoise bangle bracelets adorned her wrists.

"Rue, you look amazing as well. Love those boots. What do you call them?"

"Ariat. They're about a couple hundred years old, like me. What about the parade tomorrow?" Rue asked, undeterred by the flattery.

"Clementine has already wheedled Tripp into taking us to the parade. We'll be there." *Whether I like it or not*, she mentally added.

"I hate leaving you all alone."

"I'm not alone. My daughter is here."

"That little girl fell asleep in the middle of dinner," Rue said. "Why, her face was nearly in the spaghetti." The older woman's face softened and she offered a musing smile, her affection for the five-year-old obvious.

"Kindergarten is tough work," Hannah said with a laugh. She placed her hand on Rue's arm. "Please, stop worrying about me. I'd be absolutely miserable at a dance. I've never been one for that sort of thing."

Hannah had her fill of parties growing up. Debutante balls, soirees, and receptions were the norm at her grandmother's sprawling estate. Unlike her granddaughter, the CEO of Bryant Oil thrived on the constant social events.

She smiled as she glanced down at her T-shirt, cutoffs and flip-flops. It had been a long time since she'd worn a designer dress or had her hair and nails done and she didn't miss any of that world.

A knock at the back door had both Rue and Hannah turning.

Tripp Walker stood on the porch with his hat in his hand.

"Come on in, Tripp," Rue said.

The cowboy stepped inside, wearing his usual work uniform of faded Levi's and a plaid Western shirt rolled up to the elbows.

"Tripp isn't going to the social, either." Hannah stated the obvious. She left off the fact that she was somewhat relieved to know that he wasn't going to be dancing with all of Timber's beautiful buckle bunnies and cowgirls.

"Tripp not going to the social is a given," Rue said.

"Excuse me?" The cowboy stood in the doorway, eyes wide. "Am I in some kind of trouble?"

"Not yet," Rue said. She smiled up at him. "I had a nice chat with Chief Daniels when I was in town today. He told me the oddest thing. That you two are—"

"Don't believe everything you hear," Hannah interrupted with an adamant shake of her head.

Tripp did a double take from Hannah to Rue as panic galloped across his face. "You didn't tell anyone, did you, Rue?" he asked. "Like Dutch?"

"No, but the chief is probably going to take care of that."

"Perfect," Tripp muttered.

Rue glanced at her watch. "I'll see you two later." She offered a two-finger salute as she slipped past Tripp and out the door.

"Don't stay out too late," Hannah called after the older woman.

"Very funny, dear."

"You think she's serious?" Tripp asked as he stepped farther into the kitchen.

"About Chief Daniels? I don't know the man. You tell me."

"This is a small town, Hannah. Gossip spreads like butter on warm biscuits."

She shrugged. "Sometimes all you can do is nod and smile and let the gossip roll on past."

"That's your plan?"

"No more." She held up a hand. "I'm done with crisis intervention for a while. Could we postpone any further meltdowns until after the holiday?"

"Fine by me, so long as the grapevine doesn't have us married by Monday."

Hannah laughed. "If we are, I promise you'll be the first to know."

"You aren't taking this very seriously," he said.

"I do take this seriously, Tripp. And I haven't thanked you for coming down to the police station. Only a real friend would do that." She looked up at him. "You were willing to let people think that you and I...you know... to protect Clementine. Don't think I don't appreciate that. I do."

He nodded.

Silence filled the space between them. "May I offer you a soda?" Hannah asked, hoping to move past the awkward moment.

"Well, sure. Why not? What do you have?" Tripp asked.

"Root beer and root beer. It's my favorite."

"I'll have a root beer, please."

"Good choice." Hannah opened the refrigerator and grabbed two glass-bottled longnecks, doing her best not to chuckle. As she closed the door, Trent Blaylock and Josee Queen's save-the-date card slid down the refrigerator to the floor.

Tripp and Hannah reached for the paper at the same time.

"I got it," Tripp said as their fingers touched. He handed her the card without meeting her eyes.

"Thank you." She offered him the bottle and stepped back.

Tripp twisted off the cap and took a long pull. Hannah stared, fascinated. Something about Tripp always seemed to fascinate her.

She needed to learn to be un-fascinated ASAP because Tripp Walker was a dead end. He'd made it clear how he felt about her on too many occasions, despite their fake relationship.

When Hannah struggled with the cap on her own root beer, Tripp slipped the bottle from her fingers and twisted off the cap.

"Thank you," she murmured, holding the cold bottle to her heated face.

"So you're not going to the social tonight?" Tripp asked.

"Small talk with strangers is not my idea of fun," she said.

"Mine, either."

He rubbed his calloused thumb over the top of the bottle and met her gaze. "Mind if I ask you something?"

"I'm an open book."

"Yeah. Nice try, but I do have a question."

Hannah offered him a long, tortured sigh. "Please, go ahead."

"Why did Trent Blaylock send you flowers?"

"That was weeks ago." She took a sip of the soda and relished the cool liquid.

"Yep. Weeks ago."

"I gave him relationship advice, and he was grateful. He and Josee are now engaged."

Tripp frowned. Clearly, that was not the answer he expected.

"I never asked why you stopped by," Hannah said.

"I came to return something." He pulled a small, rolled-up spiral-bound notebook out of his back pocket.

Hannah inhaled sharply and her face lit up. "My recipe book! I've been looking for it all week." She put her root beer on the table and reached for the notebook. "Thank you so much. Where did you find it?"

"It was under the front passenger seat. I found it when I cleaned the truck."

"It must have fallen out of my purse."

"You've got some pretty interesting recipes in there." He leaned back against the cupboard and crossed his legs, looking as comfortable as can be, and took another swig.

"You looked in my personal notebook," Hannah said.

"How else would I find the owner?"

Hannah flipped through the pages. "My name isn't in here."

"There's a folded menu from the Dripping Falls Diner at the corner of Central and Fir Streets tucked in the back."

"Oh."

"Are those secret recipes?" he asked.

"They're my best recipes. My famous chili recipe is in there."

"I missed that." He reached for the notebook. "Let me see."

Hannah held it away from him. "No way. I'm entering that in the..." She slapped a hand over her mouth. "Oops."

"You're entering the chili cook-off?" He grinned like he'd just heard a joke. When he did, Hannah realized he had a small dimple in his right cheek.

She looked away and held her notebook close to her chest. "Yes. I am. Don't sound so surprised. I do cook for a living."

"Why didn't you mention that you entered?"

"It wasn't a secret."

"Then why didn't you mention it?"

"Dutch knew. Besides, it's four weeks away. I wanted to wait until closer to the competition for more impact."

Tripp chuckled. "You like competition. Admit it."

"Maybe I do." She smiled and met his gaze. "I heard that you've won the contest every year since it started."

"That might be an exaggeration since this is only the third year they've held the contest."

"Yes, but you did win. Correct?"

Tripp shrugged. "Yeah, okay, I won."

"What kind of chili are you making this year?" she asked.

He stared her down. "I can't tell you that."

"Does it bother you that I've entered the competition?"

"Bother me?" He shook his head. "Nope." Tripp opened the cupboard under the sink and put his bottle in the recycle bin. "Entry fee is pretty stiff, though. Fifty bucks."

"I already paid."

"Sounds like you're getting serious about this," he said.

"Fifty bucks is plenty to get serious about, but I don't play unless I'm going to win."

Tripp laughed. "A little full of yourself, aren't you?"

"Not at all. Where'd your prize-winning recipe come from, anyhow?" she asked.

"When I was a kid I got a job bussing tables at a diner in Oklahoma City. The owner said he used to be a Michelin-star chef. Who knew if he really was?" Tripp shrugged. "But he could cook and the old guy taught me everything he knew. Passed many of his best recipes on to me."

"That's a cool story, but I can't believe you were a kid when you started. How old were you?"

Tripp nodded. "Sixteen. I had just left home after... you know. I looked older than my age and I didn't get paid or anything. He gave me all the food I could eat and a place to sleep. Didn't ask questions, either."

Hannah's heart tightened at his words. "You and I have more in common than I would have thought," she said.

"Because we both ran away from home?"

She studied the floor tile for a minute before meeting his gaze. "How did you figure that out?"

"Wasn't all that difficult to connect the dots. You said that your grandmother put you through college, yet you showed up at Big Heart Ranch in a disreputable car that held the sum total of your life in a cardboard box, and your last job was in a diner in—"

She raised a hand to stop him. "It's Dripping Falls."

"Yeah, that's it." He met her gaze. "Why have you been running, Hannah?"

Sucking in a breath, she swallowed. All this time, and she hadn't talked to anyone about her grandmother's betrayal. Maybe it was time. Time to at least release a little of the pain of the past. After all, her grandmother couldn't hurt her anymore.

"My grandmother disowned me and started making noises about taking Clementine."

"Why?"

"Because I broke her rules." Hannah took a deep breath. "She had an inordinate number of rules. I ran off and got married after college. My grandmother said he was no-good. She was right. And the sad part is—" Hannah ran a hand over her blossoming abdomen "—I gave him a second chance and she was still right."

"Guess you won't make that mistake again."

She narrowed her gaze, offended at the cavalier comment. "This happens to be my life. It isn't funny."

"Didn't say it was, but the fact is, we either laugh or cry. The choice is yours. I've made plenty of mistakes. Some two or three times."

"Are you saying I'm in good company?"

"I'll let you figure that out for yourself. But there's no use bemoaning our past or the people in our past that did us a disservice. It's all about what you do today." He glanced around, noting the cake flour and mixing bowls on the counter. "So what *are* you doing?"

"Prep work for Sunday's cakes. You know. The cakewalk at the church."

"Cakes. Plural?"

"I've picked up a few custom orders."

"From who?"

"It's a secret."

"In case you haven't noticed, I'm sort of known for keeping my mouth shut."

"Okay, but you cannot tell anyone. I'm baking for Lucy because she claims she can't bake. And for Rue, because she says she's retired and absolutely refuses to bake." Hannah smiled. "It's a little surprising what a woman will pay for a cake."

"Does that mean you're making three cakes? Which one is Hannah Vincent entering in the cakewalk?"

"You'll have to try to figure that out yourself."

"I will."

She smiled. "No, you won't."

"We'll see." He glanced at the clock. "I gotta go. There are a few hours of daylight left. Jane is waiting for a ride and I promised her we'd work on our special routine."

"You have a special routine?"

"Yeah. Didn't you read the judging criteria?"

Hannah didn't bother to resist the urge to roll her eyes. "I guess I forgot since I wasn't actually training her."

"You're like a dog with a bone, aren't you?" he observed.

She crossed her arms and tossed him a few daggers.

"As far as I can tell, we'll nail full points for the handling portion. Jane is cooperative as a kitten. The judges come around with clipboards to evaluate the horse's demeanor and responsiveness with the trainer."

"Maneuvers, leading and riding. I saw that on the list."

"Uh-huh, and if we make it to the top ten finalists, then we start from scratch in the finals competition with more compulsory maneuvers and a freestyle performance."

"I can't see Tripp Walker doing a hotshot performance in an arena wearing a silk fringed shirt and chaps."

He laughed. "That makes two of us. For the record, I'm riding bareback without a bridle."

Her jaw sagged. "Jane's going to tolerate that?"

"Yep. You can stop by the corral sometime and watch. But stay back. Jane's partial to you and she'll want to cozy up to her favorite trainer instead of doing her job if she sees you." He chuckled at the admission. "You've spoiled that horse with your daily visits to love on her."

Hannah smiled at his admission. Was Jane really partial to her?

Her gaze met Tripp's and held for a moment. A warmth crept up her neck at the tiny spark of tenderness she saw in his eyes. It was like that night outside Jane's pen. A memory she cherished, in spite of herself.

As if he was thinking the same thing, Tripp's pupils rounded with concern before he broke the connection and quickly turned to the door.

"I'll be by early to pick up you and Clementine. Bring water and your patriotic spirit," he said in a no-nonsense tone as he pushed open the screen door.

"Yes, sir," she called after him. *And I won't even think about waxing sentimental about Tripp Walker.*

"Mr. Tripp, you won my momma's cake!" Clementine announced. She stood on the picnic table bench in a pretty red, white and blue dress with her orange hair pulled into a ponytail, blowing on a stars-and-stripes pinwheel.

"Yes, I did, Pumpkin," Tripp said with a smile for his favorite five-year-old.

Hannah eyed him as he held the cake in one hand and plastic cutlery and paper plates in the other. He placed everything on the picnic table.

"How did you know that was mine?" she asked.

"A brilliant deduction."

He stared down at her, struck by how downright irresistible she was in a blue patterned cotton sundress, with her dark hair pulled back from her face into a high ponytail. Hannah Vincent was the complete package:

smart, pretty and she didn't hesitate to speak her mind. She'd be a handful for most men.

He blinked, surprised at the thought.

"Momma, look. Miss Rue is coming. May I go in the church for face painting now? She'll watch me."

"Miss Rue may be busy eating cake," Hannah said as she helped her daughter jump down to the grassy ground beneath the beech tree.

"Dutch refuses to cut the cake right now," Rue said as she stepped up to the table. "He's already put it in a cooler in his truck before anyone can ask for a sample."

Hannah chuckled. "Are you serious?"

"Totally. He's flummoxed and proud as can be about that cake." She winked at Hannah.

"What kind of cake did you bake, Rue?" Tripp asked.

"Well, um, I…" She turned to Hannah.

"That's hummingbird cake, isn't it, Rue?" Hannah said.

"Why, yes. That's right, dear. That is definitely a hummingbird cake."

"Do you use coconut in yours?" he asked.

When Rue shot Hannah another panicked look, he burst out laughing.

"Very funny," Rue replied. "To be perfectly clear, since we are at a church gathering, I never once said I baked it. I said I'd entered a cake. That's all."

Tripp offered a slow nod of acknowledgment, doing his very best not to laugh again.

"May I go with Miss Rue, Momma?" Clementine's brown eyes pleaded with her mother.

"I'm delighted to watch Clementine for a bit. You two enjoy your dessert."

The older woman offered him a bemused smile with a twinkle in her eye that said she had the inside track on something. Tripp didn't want to go there. Not today. Things were going too well.

"Thank you, Rue," Hannah said.

"Mind if I sit down?" Tripp asked as Clementine skipped away.

"Oh, yes. Sure." Hannah quickly scooted clear to the other end of the table.

"Think you moved far enough down there?" he asked as he straddled the picnic bench.

Hannah opened her mouth and then closed it. "I was being polite."

"Ah. Right. Polite."

"So how did you know this was my cake?" she asked.

"I saw the one you made for Dutch when he was recovering. You used the same cake plate."

"Oh, very clever."

"I have my moments." Tripp eyed the pristine white double-layer cake. "That cake looks professional."

Hannah's brows shot up. "Is that a compliment?"

"Sure is. I'm wondering how you got that fancy decorating on the frosting."

"I used an offset spatula to make the striped pattern on the sides and top."

"Nice. Who taught you how to do that?" he asked.

"A friend of my grandmother's. Kind of like your chef friend."

When he opened his mouth to ask another question, she held up a hand and nodded toward the table. "Could we cut the cake? Or do you want to take yours home, too?"

"I'm all for sharing." He inspected the plate in front of him. "What kind is it?"

Hannah's mouth dropped open. "Didn't you read the description before you picked it?"

"Nope. I got here late because one of the chickens

got out. Barely had time to enter. I slapped down my money and when I found myself on a winning number, I picked the cake that I knew was safe. Yours."

Hannah's eyes rounded. "Safe?"

He crossed his arms. "Let me tell you a story."

"Okay."

"Last year I entered the picnic basket auction and mine was won by Estelle, Pastor Parr's mother-in-law." He glanced around. "Nice lady, but the woman is a gabber. Talked nonstop for two hours and asked me so many questions that I had hives by the time we were done with lunch."

Hannah smiled. "I'm not sure if I should be flattered or insulted."

"Don't read too much into it." He met her gaze. "Why weren't you at the cakewalk?"

She looked away. "I was a little nervous about the whole thing. To tell you the truth, I nearly pulled my cake from the fund-raiser."

"Why?"

"Oh, you know."

He stared at her for a moment as she twisted her hands and looked anywhere but at him. Then he understood. "Not excited about sharing cake and chatting with a stranger?"

"Correct," she murmured.

"Another reason I picked your cake."

She smiled. "Thank you, Tripp."

"Win-win for both of us." He paused. "By the way, I ran into Chief Daniels's wife as I was leaving the church hall and she congratulated me."

"What for?"

"She didn't say, but I think she was talking about you and me and our supposed relationship."

"Well, we do have a relationship. With a mustang and a 100-Day Challenge."

He nodded a greeting to the couple that walked past the picnic bench and offered Tripp and Hannah a smile. "I guess that means you haven't noticed folks walking by our table and grinning."

"This is a church picnic. There is nothing unusual about smiling people here."

"If you say so."

She stared at him for a minute before her eyes widened and a pained expression crossed her face. "Oh, I didn't even think. Is this whole situation putting a damper on your social calendar?"

"My what?"

"You know, dating."

Tripp nearly burst out laughing at the idea that he had a social calendar.

"Maybe you should let me worry about my social calendar." He shook his head. "Are we going to have cake or what?" He slid the paper plates and forks across the table. "What kind of cake did you say that is?"

"Lemon with lemon curd filling."

Tripp slowly turned the cake plate, inspecting from all angles. "Cream cheese frosting?"

Hannah made a face and scoffed. "Hardly. It's whipped mascarpone."

"Impressive."

"Thanks. I hope the cake was worth the price of the ticket."

"More than worth it."

"Exactly how much did you pay for that ticket?" she asked.

"You don't want to know. Needless to say, I won't be eating pancakes at the Timber Diner anytime soon."

"All for a good cause. Dutch says you have a few pet projects of your own for the orphanage."

"Dutch talks too much."

She pulled a cake knife and server, two fancy dessert plates, cutlery and cloth napkins from her tote bag.

"You came prepared. Is that china?" he asked.

"Yes. They're flea market finds. My one weakness. But I keep moving around, so I can't collect more than fits in the trunk of my car."

"How'd you get from Missouri to Colorado anyhow?"

"I drove an old Subaru wagon whose engine caught on fire outside of Denver."

"Not real good with vehicles, are you?"

Hannah sigh. "I have other talents."

He raised the dish and turned it over. "Excellent taste."

"A cowboy with discriminating china opinions?"

"I like a nice plate as much as the next cowboy."

"Good to know." Hannah cut the cake and slid a piece onto a dish, then pushed it across the table to Tripp. "Oh, I brought lemonade." She pulled out a thermos and plastic glasses.

"You thought of everything." He brought a forkful of cake to his mouth and paused midtaste, stunned at the flavors on his tongue. "Hannah," he said.

"Is anything wrong?"

"Are you kidding? This tastes like more."

"Excuse me?"

"*More.* That means that your cake tastes like second helpings will be in order."

"Oh, I'm so glad."

He scooped up another piece, savoring it before

slowly swallowing. When he looked up, Hannah was watching him.

"You really like it?" she asked.

"Hannah, I know horses and I know cooking. This is a masterpiece."

"A masterpiece?" She blinked and stared at him.

The way she beamed at his compliment and hesitantly smiled beneath his gaze caused a jolt of awareness to hit him. On the outside, Hannah was in your face, but inside, she was as insecure and shy as he was.

He took another bite. "Sour cream?"

Hannah blinked. "Um, what?"

"Sour cream. That's what makes the cake so moist."

"Yes." She grinned. "Yes. That's right."

"Would you consider sharing recipes?" Tripp asked.

"What do you have to offer?" She cocked her head and frowned. "I heard you don't bake."

"Not true. Baking is personal. I don't share my baking with just anyone." He picked up the last crumb of lemon curd from his plate and popped it in his mouth.

"Yet, you offered to share recipes with me?" Hannah asked.

"You're clearly a discriminating baker. I'd consider it an honor."

"Oh?" She cocked her head as if assessing his words. "So you'd share your best cake recipe if I shared mine?"

"I'll have to give that some thought," Tripp said.

"Seriously? You said my cake was a masterpiece."

"Hey, all of my cakes are my best, though I think this lemon cake might beat me in competition."

"Really?"

"Yeah, but I do have a secret carrot cake recipe that makes folks swoon. I hardly ever make it because it makes women get crazy ideas. Like I might be getting serious or something. Carrot cake doesn't say love, it says friendship."

Hannah gestured with her fork. "You know, not many people understand the language of food."

"Never thought of it that way, but you're right," Tripp said.

"And clearly," she continued, "red velvet cake is the language of love."

He looked at her. Really looked at her, realizing he'd underestimated the little baker.

"More cake?" Hannah asked.

"Oh, yeah."

Hannah crinkled her nose and flinched as she put another slice on his plate.

"Sunburn?" Tripp peered at the pink skin across the bridge of her nose.

"Yes. That was a long parade yesterday."

"Every year the Fourth of July parade gets a little longer. But it was a good time, wasn't it?"

Hannah offered a musing smile. "The best. I took a dozen pictures of Clementine on your shoulders waving her flag and laughing so hard she was near tears."

Tripp grinned. Hannah and Clementine made it fun. Once or twice he'd grabbed Hannah's hand to pull her through the crowd of tourists visiting for the holidays and she'd laugh as the three of them jockeyed for a better viewing spot along the sidewalk. A tiny place in Tripp's heart that had been closed for a long time seemed to open up yesterday.

Despite the side glances and meaningful smiles of those that he'd known for a long time, Tripp realized that there were a lot worse things in life than folks thinking he had a ready-made family.

Chapter Nine

"Why are you mucking? Aren't you supposed to be off this morning?" Tripp asked.

Hannah jumped at the words, surprised to hear Tripp outside the stall. She yanked the bandana covering her mouth and nose down and turned around. "Yes. Just like you're supposed to be on a conference call."

"I'm done. Took less time than I figured."

"Have you ever noticed that you always seem to show up when I least expect it?" she asked.

"That's my job." He frowned. "But you didn't answer my question."

"I had to cancel my doctor appointment." She picked through the shavings with the rake and dumped the unwanted stuff into the wheelbarrow. "I checked the schedule and one of the kids assigned to muck is out sick with poison ivy."

"Why?" He pointedly looked at her.

"I told you why. Poison ivy. Apparently, it's all over him." She glanced up at the row of ceiling fans. Though they continued a nonstop rhythm, the air seemed without movement in the huge facility. "Whew. Hot today, isn't it?"

"Hannah, why did you cancel your appointment? If you needed a ride, why didn't you just say so?" He swatted at a fly, growing more annoyed by the minute.

"Tripp, you've got back-to-back conference calls this morning." She swiped at her forehead with a sleeve.

"I can easily reschedule the rest of them if you need a ride."

"No way." She grabbed the wheelbarrow and backed out of the stall, nearly running Tripp over in the process.

"Hey, careful there, and I am trying to talk to you," he protested.

"Keep talking. I can hear you," she said over her shoulder. "I just need to dump this load. Did you forget that I'm supposed to be freeing up your time so you can work with Jane?"

"Hannah, we're six weeks from Fort Worth. Jane and I are doing just fine."

She stopped for a moment and looked at him. "July has absolutely flown by, hasn't it?"

Tripp's long strides had him moving ahead of the wheelbarrow and standing between her and the path to the mulch pile. "Call and un-cancel your appointment. I'll meet you at the truck in ten minutes."

Hannah released the handles and let the wheelbarrow go, then stared him down. "Ten minutes?" She grimaced and glanced down at herself. "I have to shower. I stink."

"Okay. Fifteen."

Thirty minutes later, Tripp guided the pickup truck past the sign announcing that they were entering the city limits of Pawhuska. "So where are we going?" he asked.

"The clinic off Main Street. You can drop me off." She pulled her still-damp hair into a ponytail and fastened it high on her head.

He shrugged. "I don't have anything else to do and

I've recently been upgraded to your significant other by the new teller at the Timber Bank, so I may as well go with you."

Hannah whirled around in her seat. "Significant other? What did you say to that?"

"Not a thing. Sometimes the best response is no response." He shrugged. "I'm kind of getting used to it. Besides, I don't mind being significant and I guess I'm already other."

"The only significant other I've ever had in my life turned out to be insignificant."

"Clementine's father?" he asked.

"Exactly."

"He's not in the picture?"

"Only when he smells money."

When Tripp raised his brows in question, she took a deep breath. Sharing was never easy, but Tripp deserved to know.

"He disappeared before Clementine was born as soon as he realized that I didn't have a penny to my name. After seven years of random drive-bys, he showed up again a few months ago. I'd always let him know where I was, in case he wanted to man up and be a father. I thought he deserved a second chance because of Clementine. It turned out that he had somehow found out about my grandmother's failing health, something I was not aware of, and determined that my financial situation would change. He was wrong." She let out a breath. "I did the best thing for all concerned and cut him loose."

"I'm sorry, Hannah."

"There's nothing to be sorry about. I hung on all those years because I didn't want to admit my grandmother had been right. But she was. The man gladly relinquished parental rights in return for not having to pay back child support."

He met her gaze, and she knew what was coming. "Are you still in love with him?" Tripp asked.

"When we met, I was in love with love." Hannah paused. "I'm no longer a woman who believes in happy endings and that love conquers all."

She shook her head. "Enough fairy-tale talk. The doctor awaits."

Tripp came around to the passenger side and offered a hand to assist her as she stepped from the truck. His touch was gentle as he held her arm.

A gal could get used to being treated like she was special, but Hannah knew better than to read more into it than the fact that Tripp Walker was always a cowboy gentleman.

"Maybe you should go grab a cup of coffee. There's that place on Kihekah Avenue," she said.

"Nope. I'm coming with you. You shouldn't have to do everything all by yourself. Friends support each other."

"Okay," she murmured. "But don't say I didn't warn you."

He held the door of the office to the large obstetrical practice open and let her lead the way. Inside the spacious waiting room, no less than fifteen pregnant women sat on the padded chairs in various stages of discomfort.

Tripp's eyes rounded and he did a very genuine deer-in-headlights impression. "Why are there so many pregnant women here?" he whispered.

"Think of this as a cattle station for expectant women."

"I guess so."

Every eye in the room was on the tall, lean cowboy who entered and stood awkwardly behind Hannah as she checked in. By the time she turned to find a seat, they were blatantly staring at the only man in the room.

"Ladies," Tripp said with a nod as he took off his hat.

He sat down next to Hannah and casually picked up a magazine. Flipping through the glossy pages, his eyes rounded and he blinked with surprise.

Hannah glanced over to see what he was reading. *Modern Childbirth* magazine. She bit back a laugh when he grimaced and quickly closed the periodical, placing it back on the table.

"Mrs. Vincent?" A nurse in pink scrubs with a clipboard called Hannah's name.

Tripp glanced around the room as if looking for Mrs. Vincent.

Hannah gathered her purse and stood. "Tripp, that's me. I have to go in now."

"You're Mrs. Vincent?"

"Yes," she whispered. "You knew that."

He chuckled. "I never put two and two together before. Mrs. Vincent sounds like your grandmother."

"No. Her name was Bryant."

"Sir, do you want to come in with Hannah?" the nurse asked.

"Sure," he said with an enthusiastic grin.

"I don't know if that's a good idea, Tripp," Hannah said quietly.

He took her arm. "Hey, we're buddies, right? I got this, Hannah."

"If you say so."

"First door on the left, sir. I'm going to weigh our patient first."

Hannah waited until Tripp was out of sight before

she took off her shoes, removed her earrings and watch and gingerly approached the industrial scale. The device clanged rudely as she stepped onto the black pad. She frowned as she got off the scales and entered the examination room.

"How'd it go?" Tripp asked.

"How do you think it went?" Hannah grumbled. "I'm the size of two hippos and a small elephant."

"Aw, you are not."

"I am, too. Stop being nice."

"Whoa. I've heard about those hormones from Jack Harris," he muttered. Tripp stood and walked around the room, inspecting the framed medical certificates on the wall. When he got to the wall behind him, he jerked his head back. "What is that?"

Hannah turned to see what he was referring to. "Those are a series of photos depicting the birthing process."

"With no warning label? That's just wrong. At least *National Geographic* warns the reader."

"This is a medical office." She looked at him and narrowed her gaze. "Are you okay?"

Tripp's color had paled. "I, um…"

The nurse came back in the room and grabbed the blood pressure cuff. Her gazed moved from Tripp to Hannah. "Is he okay?"

"No, he's not." Hannah placed a hand on his arm. "He's leaving to grab a cup of coffee." She squeezed his bicep. "Right now."

"That sounds like a very good idea," the nurse said. "Should I get him a wheelchair?"

Tripp held up a hand. "Not necessary. I got this."

"At least he tried," the nurse said. "Most of them

don't even try." She smiled wistfully at Tripp's retreating form. "He's one of the good guys."

Hannah stared at the nurse. She was right. Tripp was one of the good guys.

After her appointment, Hannah found Tripp pacing back and forth across the lobby with his hat in his hands. As if sensing her presence, he looked up.

"I don't know what happened to me," he said. A pained expression crossed his face. "I deliver cattle and horses all the time. But this was different. I just sort of lost it."

"It's okay, Tripp. Here, I brought you a present." She handed him a small snapshot.

"What is this?"

"My ultrasound photo. This is the baby."

"Ultrasound. We do those for horses, you know."

"Yes, I do know. Babies are different. They grow up and want an allowance and eventually ask for the keys to your car."

Tripp was oblivious to her joking words. He continued to stare, mesmerized, at the photo, turning it around to different angles. "Look at that. You can see the little fingers and toes and all."

Hannah grimaced. "Ooh, ouch. The baby just kicked me."

"What?"

Hannah took his palm and placed it on her abdomen. "Feel that?" She had his full attention now.

Tripp's gaze met hers and the blue eyes widened. "*I felt that.* The baby kicked. Unbelievable."

"Oh, it's believable at 3:00 a.m. Trust me." She hooked her arm through his. "Now, do you mind if I pick up my prenatal vitamins at the drugstore before we head back to Timber?"

"Not a problem. I canceled everything for the morning."

"That means tomorrow will be even busier."

"It's fine. I never take any time off and you haven't since you arrived on Big Heart Ranch."

They pushed through the glass doors of the clinic and started down the street.

"Look," Hannah said. She nodded to the left. They stood in front of a small infant and children's shop. A white crib with pink polka-dot decor had been set up in the window. Small bubbles of joy released in Hannah's heart. For the first time in a long time, she was excited instead of worried about her upcoming delivery.

"Pink polka dots?" Tripp scoffed. "What if you have a dirt-loving cowboy?"

Hannah leaned close. "I'll let you in on a secret. I'm having a little cowgirl and she's going to love pink and dirt."

"I thought you didn't want to know."

"No one told me. I just know."

"You just know, huh? Have you thought about names?"

"Yes. Anne. After my mother."

"That's really nice, Hannah." A soft smile crossed his face. "Really nice." He glanced at the sign on the shop's door. "Do you want to go in?"

"Could we?"

"Sure, why not?"

"You really don't mind going in there?"

"This looks a whole lot easier than that doctor's office." He reached for the door. Musical chimes sang a nursery rhyme as they entered the shop.

"Hello there. How may I assist you?" the young clerk asked.

"Oh, we're only looking," Hannah said.

"When is your baby due?" The woman's gaze went from Tripp to Hannah.

"December," Hannah said.

"Your first?"

"This is number two," Tripp answered. "Pretty exciting, huh?"

"Yes. Congratulations." The clerk smiled and handed them pink-and-blue lollipops with the store name on a clear cellophane wrapper. "Let me know if I can help with anything."

When she walked away, Hannah dared to look up at Tripp.

He shrugged and offered a sheepish grin. "Sorry. I opened my mouth and it came out, and then I got carried away."

Hannah laughed. "Don't apologize to me. I'm fine with it, as long as you don't mind being accused of being the baby daddy."

"I've been accused of worse." He glanced at a neat stack of blankets. "These are kind of thin—what are they for?"

"Receiving blankets. You swaddle the baby with them."

"Swaddle?"

"Wrap them tightly. It's comforting for the baby."

"Swaddle. Got it." He nodded to another item on the shelf. "And this?"

"Thermal carrier."

"To keep the baby warm? Seems a little small."

Hannah broke out in giggles, which brought a look from the clerk. "No, it's to keep the baby's bottle warm."

"Right. That makes sense." He turned and inspected a shelf of infant T-shirts. "What have you gotten for the new baby?"

"Nothing. Not yet. I don't even know where I'll be in December."

"What do you mean, nothing? Your baby is coming, Hannah." Tripp seemed genuinely distressed with her answer.

"I have plenty of time. The only thing I'm certain of is that I'll be at Big Heart Ranch until the 100-Day Mustang Challenge is completed."

"And then what? You don't have to leave the ranch, you know."

"I can't live in a bunkhouse with a baby and a five-year-old forever. I need a place of my own. I don't want to have to move twice."

"Clementine will have started first grade by early September," he said. "That's coming right up."

"I know, Tripp. I know. Try to understand that a part of me just doesn't want to think about all the decisions I have to make just yet." She tugged on his arm. "Come on. Let's go. I have to get my prescription."

He held the door for her as they left the shop and stepped out onto the sidewalk. "Mind if I run an errand while you get your vitamins?" he asked.

"Of course not."

He handed over his key fob. "I'll meet you at the truck."

"You can meet me all you want, but I'm never going to be able to get into that truck." She patted her abdomen. "At least not without help."

He chuckled. "There's a bench on the sidewalk where we parked. I'll meet you there."

"Okay."

Hannah stood in line to pick up her prescription. On the way out, she heard her name called and looked around. Standing next to the candy aisle was AJ Maxwell.

"AJ! What are you up to?"

"Ogling chocolate I'm not supposed to have while my husband is bringing the truck around."

"You're due any day now, right?"

"Yes. Travis is helping me run errands. I'm no longer allowed to drive."

"The doctor won't let you drive?"

"No. Travis won't let me drive."

Hannah chuckled at the words.

AJ rubbed a hand over her stomach. "I sure hope this baby is punctual. I'm ready to have my body back."

"I hear you." Hannah laughed.

"What are you doing?"

"My car died, so Tripp took me to the doctor."

"Oh, my. That is so sweet. Someone told me you two were close."

Hannah held up a hand and shook her head. "No, it's not like that. I know there's sort of a rumor going around about us, but we're just friends."

"Oh, yes. I understand. Tripp and I are friends, too. He was one of the most welcoming and supportive people at the ranch when I showed up." AJ smiled. "But he looks at you a tad bit different than he looks at his other friends."

"Tripp only looks at me like he wants to give me a piece of his mind." Hannah released an awkward laugh. "And then he generally does."

The blonde gave a slow shake of her head. "Not true, Hannah. Maybe you should open your eyes. That cowboy is smitten." AJ glanced at her watch. "Uh-oh, I promised to be outside."

"See you back at the ranch," Hannah said, still dumbfounded by the other woman's remarks.

"Yes." AJ reached out to catch Hannah in a hug. "Good to see you."

Hannah paid for her vitamins and headed out of the store, still pondering AJ's words. The morning sunshine was already blinding and hot. Hannah slipped on her sunglasses and looked down the street. There was Tripp, waiting on the bench under a store canopy.

He stood and smiled when he saw her.

Smitten?

"How come I beat you back to the truck?" he asked.

"I ran into AJ. We were chatting. She and Travis are running errands today."

"You all right? You sound odd," he asked as he helped her into the truck.

"I'm fine." Hannah glanced into the back seat of the cab as she fastened her seat belt. She did a double take. The entire back seat was filled with pink polka-dot shopping bags. "Tripp, what is that?"

He grinned and looked at her. There was a glint of humor in his eyes. "I had so much fun at that baby shop, I went back and picked up a few things."

A few things? Hannah was stunned silent. It was all she could do to close her gaping mouth.

"What do you think?" Tripp asked.

"What are they for?"

He looked at her like she was a few heifers short of a herd. "*For your baby.* You said a girl, right?"

She nodded numbly.

"Don't worry. That clerk said to keep the tags and you can return anything that doesn't work for little baby Anne."

Hannah stared at him.

"Hot in here." He started the truck. "Let's get that air conditioner cranked up."

"Thank you," she murmured.

Tripp turned at her words and peered closely, blue eyes filled with concern. "Hey, there. Are you sure you're okay?"

"I'm speechless."

"I'm sure it's only temporary." He chuckled. "By the time we're home, you'll be back to giving me what for."

An unfamiliar ache welled up inside of Hannah.

Home. By the time they were home.

She stared at his strong profile, knowing that she was very much in danger of forgetting that she didn't believe in happy endings and losing her heart to this stubborn, unpredictable and generous cowboy anyhow.

"What do you think?" Tripp asked. The sun had begun its slow descent as he turned from the center of the pen toward Hannah. She had been sitting on a folding chair under a tree for hours while he went through the steps of the judging routine with Jane.

"I'm impressed." She stood and stretched before walking up to the pen. "You said Jane was having issues with the side pass and pivot. I thought she ran through everything like a pro."

"You think she's weak in any area?"

"Tripp, honestly, this horse is amazing and so is her trainer. Aren't you going to show me your freestyle performance?"

"It's getting late and I've kept you from your daughter long enough."

"Jane has to get used to an audience," Hannah countered.

"I've been running through it with the music and all with the kids watching over at the girls' ranch. They have a better sound system there. Jane can handle an audience. And we have it nailed down to the three and a half minutes required."

"I'm sorry I missed that."

"It's a not fancy show like some of those trainers will have, but it's a solid performance that will demonstrate this horse is special. Maybe I'll get a judge who favors simplicity over grandstanding."

Tripp opened the gate and locked it behind himself. "Did I remember to tell you that Lucy's sending me to a two-day conference in Tulsa next week? You're going to be in charge."

"Only twice already and it's on the calendar."

"Did I? Well, the big alumni barbecue and rodeo will be over by then."

"And the chili cook-off, too," she said with a grin.

"My point here is that things will have returned to normal. Whatever that is."

"You're only gone for two days and a night. I can handle it."

"You're also five months pregnant."

"Don't start that again. I've been here since late May. Surely you trust me by now."

"Not about trust. I trust you, Hannah. You know that."

Jane whinnied loudly as if to tell them to stop bickering.

"Look at her," Hannah said. Awe laced her voice. "It's horse ballet," she whispered.

They were silent for a few moments. In the pen Jane danced across the dirt, her copper mane flying as she showed off, enjoying the audience.

Tripp turned and leaned back against the fence, his eyes on Hannah.

"She's so lovely," she murmured.

"Yeah," he agreed, his attention focused on the woman next to him. A soft breeze fluttered the trees overhead. Instead of the usual humidity, tonight the temperature had dropped a tad as though Mother Nature was as tired of summer as everyone else.

When Hannah's hair blew into her face, he was unable to resist leaning closer to gently brush the strands from her cheek. Their gazes met and held, and somehow Tripp closed the distance between them.

Hannah's lashes fluttered downward as he bent his head until his lips grazed hers, hesitantly until he realized she was kissing him back. Then Tripp was helpless to do anything but take her in his arms and deepen the kiss until he was lost in the sweetness and rightness of the moment. It was as if his whole life he'd been waiting for that kiss and this woman.

It was Hannah who stepped out of his arms. He watched her closely, but she just stood there. Her eyes were round, and she held her fingers to her mouth as if she was as stunned as he was.

What just happened? Why is my heart ramming up against my ribs and my breath catching in my throat?

Tripp opened his mouth to say something, but he didn't know what to say. It wasn't like he had a mental saddlebag filled with things to say to a woman after he kissed her. Fact was, his saddlebag was pretty much empty. Apparently, his mind was, too. Yet, there was no way he wished it hadn't happened.

"I'm not sure if I should apologize or say thank you," he finally said.

Hannah finally blinked and looked at him. "I don't know what to say to that."

"Not much to say," he admitted.

Tripp's phone began to buzz, and the sound startled him, pulling him out of his reverie.

"Mine's buzzing, too," Hannah said.

"That can't be good," Tripp said as he pulled his phone out of his pocket.

"AJ," Hannah said, glancing at the screen of her cell. "She had a boy."

"Travis Jake Maxwell." Tripp grinned and shook his head.

"Oh, my, this is so wonderful."

"Yep, and I'm guessing that kid will be as funny-looking as his parents."

"I heard Travis was on the cover of *Tulsa Now* magazine a while back. Gosh, and AJ looks like a model. Their baby is going to be beautiful."

"I was kidding, Hannah." He shook his head. "The irony here is that Travis was burned so badly in the past, he was dead set against relationships. Until AJ came along. He fell hard and fast."

"I suppose you can't plan for everything, can you?" she said softly without looking at him.

"No. I guess not."

When the breeze blew Hannah's hair again, Tripp clenched his hands at his sides. She nodded toward the bunkhouse.

"Rue is watching Clementine. I better go."

"Yeah." He nodded.

Hannah turned from him and then stopped and pivoted right back around. "Don't apologize," she said with a determined look in her eye. "That was a very good kiss."

His lips twitched as she walked away. Yeah, she was right. It was a very good kiss. Behind him, Jane nickered. When Tripp didn't turn, she bumped into the fence and nearly knocked off his hat with a nudge from her nose. He finally turned and met the mare's velvet brown eyes.

Tripp released a long breath. "Yeah, I know. She likes us. Now all we have to do is find a way to make her stay."

Chapter Ten

"**D**id you ever smell anything so amazing?"

Hannah turned at Tripp's voice. She'd been trying to ignore his presence in the small exhibitor tent to her left for the last few hours. Though the tent canopy was down on that side, she still caught glimpses of him and found herself thinking about that kiss last night.

She'd lost sleep over that kiss. Well, she certainly did not intend to lose the Big Heart Ranch chili competition over it. Maybe that was his strategy.

It wasn't going to work.

"Hey, anyone home over there?" he persisted.

"Were you speaking to me?" Hannah asked. She lifted the side flap on her tented booth and glanced over at him ever so nonchalantly. The man looked like Clint Eastwood in an apron. Tall and lean and all cowboy, minus the cowboy hat today. And apparently cooking brought out the best in him because he was grinning as he stirred a giant cast-iron pot.

"Who else would I be talking to?" he asked. "My competitor on the left is Mrs. Hagwood, the retired town librarian, and she's profoundly deaf. I have to keep going over to her tent to tell her that her phone is ringing."

"Good for her. No interruptions while she's cooking."

"I guess." Tripp shrugged. "But you still didn't answer my question."

He carefully wiped the edge of his pot with a paper towel. Hannah inched closer to look at his tent. The place was immaculate. She frowned as she glanced around her slightly disorganized cooking table, strewn with spices and over to the corner of the tent, where Clementine sat on the ground coloring in a book. Well, she was a free spirit. Nothing wrong with that.

She looked back at Tripp somewhat confused. "I'm sorry, could you repeat the question?"

"Never mind. It was rhetorical."

"I see." Hannah inhaled deeply. The chili cook-off was into its third hour, enough time to allow the enticing blend of sausage, beef, tomatoes and spices to mingle and create a potent aroma. "It really smells amazing now that everyone's chili is simmering, doesn't it?"

He stared at her and chuckled.

"What?"

"Nothing. Inside joke." He nodded toward the stove. "Ever cooked on a camp stove before?"

"I have not and I must admit that there has been a bit of a learning curve."

"Hi, Mr. Tripp," Clementine called. She peeked around Hannah and waved.

"Clementine. I didn't know you were there. What are you doing?"

"Coloring." She looked at her mother. "Momma, I'm hungry."

"She can have some of my chili," Tripp called.

"Or we can borrow your mini-me and take her for

hot dogs and curly fries," Dutch said as he approached her booth with Rue.

"Hot dogs," Clementine said. Her eyes lit up.

Hannah frowned at the exchange.

"Dear, let us take Clementine," Rue said.

"Please, Momma," Clementine pleaded.

"Dutch and I will take good care of her," Rue continued. "We're on our way to find something to eat right now."

"Rue, you're always helping me out. I don't want to take advantage of you."

"Think of us as honorary grandparents. We get to wind her up and tire her out. Then we give her back to you. It's a wonderful arrangement."

"Yeah, and we're real good at it," Dutch said.

"If you're sure," Hannah said.

"Very sure. Are there any special stops we should make along the way?" Rue asked.

"Clementine wants to watch Dub Harris in the greased pig competition and she wants to ride a burro."

"I do believe we can handle that," Dutch said.

Hannah glanced at her watch. "I didn't think about the time factor when I signed up for this. It's pretty much an all-afternoon event." She sighed. "I was in a rush to sign up so I could beat Tripp."

"Understandable," Dutch said with a glance over at Tripp.

"We'll be back later to see who wins," Rue said.

"To see me win," Hannah added.

"I heard that," Tripp called. "My chili is ready for tasting. Is yours?"

Hannah grabbed the wooden spoon and stirred her own velvety mixture. "Mine is, as well."

Next door, Tripp positioned a mason jar in a prominent position near his cutlery and napkins.

"What's he doing over there?" Hannah whispered to Dutch.

"A little side fund-raising. That's a donation jar to raise money for the Pawhuska Orphanage."

"I thought the chili was free. Take a scorecard, sample chili and turn it in," Hannah said.

"Sure, it's free. They pay money to get in the gate. Tripp there is utilizing a little free enterprise. Hit 'em hard and hit 'em fast while their taste buds are dancing."

"Two can play at that game," Hannah said. "I need you to go to my bunkhouse and bring me the two Texas sheet cakes that are on the counter."

"You made cakes?"

"I was going to just put them on the buffet table but I can see I've been approaching this all wrong."

"Let's see who raises more money for the orphanage," Dutch said with a grin.

"Exactly."

"How much are you going to charge for each piece?"

"I'm not going to charge. I'm going to take donations." She nodded to her left. "Just like he's doing."

"Yee-haw. Let the games begin."

With the appearance of the cake, Hannah was suddenly so busy she almost didn't have time to think about Tripp being next door. The line to her tent rivaled Tripp's line. After scooping up chili samples, she continued to cut cakes.

Yet, despite being busy, she was aware of him and caught herself peeking a glance over at the other tent watching him interact with his friends and neighbors and offer a greeting and a smile. This was a Tripp that wasn't seen very often, she was certain. He liked people much more than he let on and enjoyed their approval.

Occasionally, his gaze met hers and he'd smile, and her heart would catch and she'd forget what she was doing.

"Hannah," Tripp called out hours later.

"What?" She pulled off her plastic gloves and grabbed a bottle of water. Turning toward his tent, she met the blue eyes assessing her with respect and a hint of something else she couldn't put her finger on. *Interest?*

"They're announcing the cook-off winners over at the main podium. We can hear it from here."

"Oh, that means we're done." Hannah leaned against the table with relief and glanced around her. The chili was nearly gone and all that remained of the cake was crumbs. Hannah absently swiped her finger along an empty sheet cake tray and tasted bits of delicate chocolate cake. Absolutely delicious, even if she was a bit biased.

She looked over at Tripp's tent. He was neatly stacking up his kettles and utensils.

"Your pot is empty?" she asked.

"Uh-huh. They cleaned me out. But I saved you a cup of chili. Want to trade?"

"Yes. I'm starving. And, of course, I want to taste your prize-winning chili."

"You want to try to figure out the ingredients," Tripp said.

Hannah bit back a laugh. "That, too."

Tripp pulled off his apron and closed the distance between the booths. He offered her a paper cup with a spoon and glanced around her tent. "Any cake left?" he asked hopefully.

"No, sorry."

"That's a shame."

She scooped up a sample of her chili and handed it to him before she took the cup he offered. "Mine is not vegetarian."

He shrugged. "It's okay. I'll work around it."

Hannah dug her spoon into his chili and lifted it to her mouth. "*Oh, this is good.* This is very good."

"Yeah?" He laughed. "Maybe you could try not to sound so surprised."

She tasted again and frowned, closing her eyes for a moment as she separated the flavors in her mind.

"You're frowning."

"No, I'm analyzing. Is that sweet potato in there? And do I taste a bit of cumin?"

"Right on all counts."

"Black beans and lentils," she added.

"Well done, chef."

"What kind of chilies?"

"Ancho, pasilla and arbol." He paused. "And maybe a hint of chipotle."

"Oh, Tripp, this is a winner. I'd really like the recipe."

"We can negotiate." He raised his brows. "When you bake another cake."

She chuckled at his response.

Overhead, a microphone screeched and squealed. "Big Heart Ranch's own Tripp Walker wins the chili cook-off. Second place goes to Hannah Vincent, also of Big Heart Ranch."

"Congratulations," Hannah said with a slight bow of deference. "Well deserved."

"Second place is pretty good for your first year," Tripp said.

"I am not a sore loser. In fact, I am delighted to have had the opportunity to compete against you." Hannah grabbed the glass jar and started counting the cake donations.

"That's the spirit. How much money do you have in that jar?"

"Give me a minute." She finished counting the change and dumped it all back in. "Two thousand and fifty-one dollars and ten cents."

Tripp's jaw sagged. "What? You're kidding me, right?"

"No. I'm serious."

"How many pieces of cake were there?"

"Fifty-six."

His eyes rounded. "You charged thirty-six dollars for each piece of cake?"

Hannah blinked. "That was some impressive math. But no, I took donations, just like you. AJ was right—people do open up their pocketbooks for the pregnant lady."

She handed the jar to Tripp.

"Why are you giving it to me?"

"It's for the Pawhuska Orphanage. I trust you'll get this to the appropriate parties."

"Hannah, that was unbelievably cool of you to do that."

"I happen to be an unbelievably cool person. It's taken you three months to figure that out?" She nodded toward his donation jar. "How much did you rake in with your chili samples?"

"Couple hundred bucks." He frowned. "Maybe I should bake cakes," he said.

"Your chili also won a hundred bucks and that will go to the orphanage."

"Two thousand dollars?" he repeated.

She nodded. "You won the pots and pans and the gift certificate to the Oklahoma Rose. Not a bad haul."

"I'm particular about the tools of my trade. I always give the ones I win back. They've been trying to give away those skillets for three years now."

Hannah laughed at the notion.

"Is Clementine still with Rue and Dutch?" he asked.

"No. She's sleeping." Hannah pointed to the blanket pallet on the floor of the tent. "They claim they wore her out. Although I suspect she wore them out."

She began to collect her own pots and utensils.

"The cook-off was a lot more fun than usual," Tripp said, giving her a meaningful glance. "We should compete more often."

Hannah smiled. "Should we?"

"Yeah. I don't know many people who take their horses and their cooking as seriously as I do."

"Did you just compliment me?"

He granted her a rare full-on smile. "You know, I might have."

She was silent, pondering his words as she cleaned up the booth. "Will you keep an eye on Clementine while I run this stuff up to the bunkhouse?"

"Happy to. Are you coming back for the fireworks later? There's rumor of a s'mores booth."

"That sounds wonderful. But I've been on my feet all day. I'm exhausted. And my daughter is a lightweight like me."

"Sure," he said with a nod. "I'm not much of a s'mores fella anyhow. If I can't have Hannah Vincent's cake, I'd rather go hungry."

"I guess there's some baking in my future. It's good to keep the boss happy."

"Now don't feel like you have to do it on my account."

She laughed as she collected trash from the tent and walked it over to a receptacle. "Will someone be breaking down the tent and collecting the camp stoves?"

"Yeah. There's a crew that will do all that."

"Then I'm done here. I'll be right back." She grabbed the rolling cart she'd borrowed from the chow hall and put everything on the shelves.

The day had begun to slow down. The rodeo was over and families were moving toward home. They'd come back in a few hours for fireworks at the pond or watch them while sitting on blankets on their lawns.

The bunkhouse was quiet. Rue would be back in her apartment in Timber tonight, now that the summer was over. Hannah put the leftover chili and sour cream and cheese in the fridge and dumped the dirty dishes and pans on the counter.

Heading back to the tent, she opened the back door. Across the grass strode Tripp with Clementine in his arms. The little girl was still asleep.

The picture they made of the tall cowboy, his face partially covered by his hat and her little girl nestled in his arms, plucked at her heartstrings.

She held open the screen door for him. "You didn't have to."

"Sure, I did. It's okay to let your friends help you."

Yes, but there was a price to pay for getting accustomed to Tripp Walker helping her all the time. She'd get used to it, maybe even expect it, and that wasn't a good idea when she had plans to head back to Dripping Falls next month.

"You can put her on this bunk."

"That little girl needs pink boots," Tripp murmured as he laid her down on the bed.

"Little girls grow out of boots much too quickly for that."

Hannah pulled off Clementine's boots and socks and tucked her beneath the sheet.

She went back into the kitchen where Tripp waited. "Thank you."

He stared at her and she was only too aware of the chili stain on her shirt and the blobs of sour cream on her pants. Her hair was a lopsided sagging ponytail now, and she smelled like pork sausage and tomato sauce.

"Yes, I know I look like I've been slinging chili for eight hours."

"Nope. I was thinking you look lovely."

Hannah blinked and leaned against the counters, speechless. She nervously tucked a loose strand of hair back behind her ear.

"Why are you surprised?" he asked.

"I, um, my physical appearance is just not something I've ever thought much about."

"And yet, you are a beautiful woman. Inside and out."

"Thank you," she murmured.

"I'm glad you came to Big Heart Ranch. Your strength and Godliness is an inspiration to everyone."

"Where did that come from?" Hannah asked.

"I don't know. I've been watching you all day today and it sort of hit me. You give two hundred percent to everything you do and you do it selflessly." A small smile touched his face. "Five months pregnant and you've been on your feet all day serving chili, *and* you raised a small fortune for the Pawhuska Orphanage."

"Oh, that's only because I was trying to beat you."

Tripp smiled before he crossed the room. He gently

took her face in his hands and pressed a soft kiss to her forehead like she was cherished and precious. "Thank you, Hannah."

And then he was gone and Hannah was left staring at the door, her heart pounding as she realized she'd fallen in love with Tripp Walker.

"Cold, rainy and plain disagreeable," Dutch muttered as he stomped into the stables and parked himself outside the office door.

Hannah turned at Dutch's words.

"What's wrong?" she asked.

"Don't ever get old. That's all I'm gonna say. Though for the record, I'm not just old, I'm two years older than dirt. This weather makes everything ache."

"Well, go on home, then," she said.

"Naw, it's Friday. I'll see the day out."

Hannah finished filling out the September supply list and turned off her computer. Dutch was right. It had been a miserable few days of weather with nonstop rain. But the horses loved the moisture and the drop in temperatures that came with the end of summer.

September was days away, along with the 100-Day Challenge finale. She planned to go to Fort Worth, Texas, to cheer Tripp and Jane on with Clementine, Lucy, Travis and Dutch. Hannah glanced at the calendar, counting down the days. When it was over, she'd have to make some serious decisions about her future.

But not today. Today, despite the weather, everything was just fine in her world. If she had any more days like today, she would be inclined to stay.

She stood and stretched before stepping out of the office to find Dutch. The wrangler stood in the center aisle, untacking a horse.

"Dutch, I keep telling you. Go home," she said. "Everything is done here. It's almost Friday quitting time anyhow."

"Naw, I can't. I promised Tripp I'd keep an eye on you while he was gone." Dutch froze with a saddle in his hands. He closed his eyes and scrunched them tight and then opened them. "You didn't hear that."

"He doesn't trust me." Hannah's heart fell flat at Dutch's words. Things had been going so well while Tripp was in Tulsa. She'd been buoyed with confidence at the thought that he left her in charge.

"No, Hannah." Dutch tossed the saddle onto the stall hook. "That's not it. Maybe when you first got here. But not now."

The heat of embarrassment warmed her face. She was humiliated in front of Dutch and becoming more annoyed with each passing moment. What a fool she had been, yet again believing that Tripp trusted her. He'd told her no less than three times that he was going out of town. In return, she'd assured him all would be well in his absence.

She thought they had an understanding.

"I should have known it was too good to be true," Hannah murmured.

"Now stop that. Did you ever think that maybe our Tripp asked me to keep an eye out because he cares about you? Come on now, you're pushing six months pregnant."

"I'm not mad at you, Dutch. You're caught in the middle."

"Go ahead and be mad at me. I should have told him no."

"The subject is closed," she said. "I'm going to go

spend some time with Jane." She grabbed her rain slicker from the hook outside the office and strode past Dutch.

"Outside the pen, right?"

"Now you sound just like Tripp," she called over her shoulder.

"That was plain rude, Missy."

"Yes, well, it is what it is."

"Don't be shooting the messenger. I'm only doing my job."

Hannah shrugged into her slicker and pulled the hood up, tucking her hair inside. She spared a glance at the gray sky overhead. The steady rain had stopped and had turned into an annoying drizzle. Wiping the moisture from her face, she called Jane.

The horse trotted to the fence and offered a welcoming whinny.

"Good to see you, too, sweet girl." She rubbed Jane's mane and offered her an apple from lunch. "Come on, let's get some walking in."

Together they walked around the pen, stopping at intervals until Hannah was tired out. "Sorry, Jane. I'm a slacker, I know. This whole pregnancy thing has me winded faster."

Hannah climbed to the top rung on the fence, leaned in and put her arms around Jane. She rested her head upon Jane's neck and inhaled, finding the peace that she always did with the mare.

"What are you doing?"

Startled, Hannah nearly lost her balance.

The next thing she knew, she'd been grabbed under the arms and set on the ground.

Tripp was back.

Hannah slowly turned to face him. "Jane needed some love," she murmured. *And I did, too*, she silently added.

"Don't ever let me see you on that fence like that again," he thundered. Tripp was angry. Steam was practically coming out of his ears. He was mad enough that Jane whinnied and raised her head in alarm.

In a heartbeat, her joy at seeing him again was replaced by confusion. He stared at her as if he didn't know her. Didn't want to know her.

Tripp Walker apparently ran hot and cold. Was this the same man who had kissed her so tenderly just a few days ago?

His eyes were a stormy blue. He stood straight and unyielding, rigid with irritation. Rain dripped from the brim of his hat as he pinned her with his gaze.

"You're scaring Jane," Hannah said. She folded her arms across her chest and stepped right into Tripp's personal space, unwilling to let him know that he scared her, as well.

"Jane is a wild mustang and what you just did was reckless. You have a child and a baby to think about, Hannah."

"I think we established weeks ago that Jane isn't like other horses. Jane is special. And I think we also established that I am a responsible adult who would never put her child in danger."

Dutch was suddenly at her side. "My fault, boss. This whole thing is completely my fault."

"Dutch, stop that," Hannah said. "I take full credit for what I did. You had nothing to do with this."

Tripp looked at them both, then as suddenly as he'd stormed in, turned on his heels and headed into the stables without so much as a backward glance.

"He's in a mood," Dutch said.

"Tripp around?"

Both Hannah and Dutch turned at the voice. It was

the tall, thin cowboy she'd seen in Timber. There was something menacing about the man. Hannah instinctively stepped back.

"Slats Milburn," Dutch echoed. "What are you doing here? How'd you get past the front gate?"

"Someone going out let me in."

"Well, that was a mistake," Dutch said. "Any business you have should be done in the admin building."

Slats nodded to Hannah. "You must be Hannah Vincent."

She ignored the hand he offered.

"Slats Milburn. I've heard a lot about you," he continued.

"That's unfortunate," Hannah murmured. She turned away and stood at the fence. Why did she have the feeling that things were about to implode?

"What are you doing here?" Dutch demanded.

"I've got business with your equine manager."

"No way does Tripp have business with you. I would have heard."

"Guess you weren't privy to this information. I'm here to meet with him because he said he was ready to settle up."

"Dutch, show him into my office," Tripp called from the doorway of the stables."

"Yes, sir, boss."

When Dutch rejoined her at the fence, Hannah asked, "What's going on, Dutch? Why was he here?"

"You got me. I don't have a clue. He closed the office door. Shot me a *mind your own business* look." Dutch shook his head. "Something ain't right, Hannah."

Hannah shoved her hands into her pockets as the rain began to fall in earnest. She shivered. Dutch was correct. Something was not right.

Chapter Eleven

"You're an heiress."

Hannah swiveled around in her desk chair, stunned by the accusation. It wasn't so much the words but the delivery. Tripp Walker might as well have accused her of being a horse thief for all the hostility that laced his words.

He stood in the doorway of the office looking larger than life and just as formidable. She hadn't seen the man since he'd voiced his displeasure with her on Friday. He'd even avoided her at church.

This morning he stepped in and closed the door behind him before he sat down. His face was a stony mask, revealing nothing. There was a calm about him that frightened her.

"Who told you that?" Hannah gripped the arms of the desk chair and braced herself for the storm that was no doubt coming. She'd lived through worse, she reminded herself.

"Dorothy Lee Bryant was your grandmother."

"Yes." She said the word slowly.

"Dorothy Lee Bryant of Bryant Oil," he stated, his voice flat and cold.

"I know who she is. She raised me."

"Why didn't you tell me?"

"I mentioned it the first day I arrived at Big Heart Ranch when I spoke with all the Maxwells." She scrambled, her mind searching. "At the obstetrician's office, too. Remember? I said my grandmother's last name was Bryant."

"Hannah, you never made it clear that you are the sole heir to the Bryant fortune. I would have remembered if my employee told me that her grandmother was one of the richest women in the country." He crossed his arms over his chest. "Why did you hide such important information?"

"I didn't hide anything. It wasn't relevant because I had already walked away seven years ago." She stared at him. Clearly, he'd missed his calling. Tripp would have made an excellent defense attorney.

"You may have walked away, but that doesn't alter the fact that you are Hannah Bryant."

"No. I'm Hannah Vincent. And why does it matter so much? I stopped being Hannah Bryant a very long time ago." She met his gaze, searching for something that told her the Tripp she knew was still there, somewhere.

He looked past her as if she wasn't in the room. "Everything you've said has been twisted tales and lies."

"That isn't true at all." She stared at him, trying to figure out where this hostility was coming from.

"Where did you say you went to college?" he asked.

"What does that matter?"

"You said you worked in equine clinics when you were a kid and when you were in college."

"I didn't lie, if that's what you're asking."

"You worked with thoroughbreds. In rich folk's stables."

"I worked with horses."

"And who taught you to bake those fancy cakes?"

"You're blowing this out of proportion, Tripp. I said it was a friend of my grandmother. Eric Frombeau taught me to bake cakes."

He blinked, processing the information. "That chef on television who bakes for movie stars?"

"Chefs on television have friends, too." She gestured with a hand. "What's your point, Tripp?"

"I'm a fool, that's my point. I marveled at how much we had in common. But we don't have anything in common. Nothing at all, do we?"

"Tripp, it was you who judged me the moment you saw me in that disreputable Honda in the middle of a storm on the side of the road. I've been honest about everything."

"You never said you were an heiress."

Hannah felt her own anger beginning to rise. "*Stop saying that.* I didn't mention who my grandmother was because she was not part of my life."

"Your life? You walked away from your life and you're pretending to be someone else."

The irony of the situation didn't fail to slap her in the face and it stung.

"That's sort of like the pot calling the kettle black, isn't it? You walked away from your life as well, didn't you?" She offered a bitter laugh. "I walked away from my grandmother's life to find my life." Hannah sighed, suddenly weary. "I thought you of all people would understand. I thought you knew me. Apparently, I was wrong."

"Nothing you say makes sense, Hannah. Your grandmother was a powerful woman. She could have found you and Clementine if she wanted to."

"Yes. I'm sure she could have. So I stayed off the grid and under the radar at all times. I moved a lot. Dripping Falls is the longest I've lived anywhere. I lived there for six months before I came here." She released a slow breath. "And maybe I didn't share more because I was ashamed."

"Your grandmother really threatened to take Clementine?"

"The threat was unspoken. But it was real. She took me away from my mother after I was born, and I always knew she would take Clementine if she so desired."

He seemed caught off guard by that bit of information and for a moment, silence stretched between them, with only the noises of the stable that drifted through the glass, breaking the tension in the room.

"You never told me that about your mother."

"Maybe because I was ashamed about that, too. I should have fought harder to find my mother before she died." Hannah stared at Tripp as the pieces of the puzzle began to fit together. Suddenly, she realized how he found out about her grandmother. "That man. Did you hire that Slats person?"

Tripp grimaced. "Yes."

His answer was like a physical blow, and Hannah flinched at the pain. "He shared information about my past with you." She paused. "I thought we were…close. I trusted you and I would have answered any question you asked. But you didn't ask. You went behind my back."

Emotion flashed in his eyes before he answered.

Hannah felt some relief that perhaps, finally, her words were getting through to him.

"It wasn't like that, Hannah. I hired him a long time ago. When you first arrived. And then I fired him. He called and told me that he had information about you.

I was concerned that it could compromise Clementine, so I agreed to hear him out."

"This is why you were so angry on Friday."

"Yes. That and seeing you with Jane."

"What exactly did he tell you?" Hannah asked.

"He said you inherited a fortune from your grandmother. That you could buy and sell Big Heart Ranch if you wanted to."

"That's not a secret. I hope you didn't pay him too much for that."

"Is it true?"

"It's absolutely true. But what he didn't tell you is that I turned it down. I walked away. That's not my money." She shook her head. "All I ever wanted was my grandmother's attention and unconditional love. The same thing my mother wanted."

He stared at her. "I don't know who you are anymore."

She met his gaze. "Funny, because that's exactly how I feel about you."

"None of this makes sense. You could take care of your children with that money."

"Bryant Oil is not my money. Even if I wanted to claim the estate, my grandmother's will has strings attached in order to control my life even from the grave."

"What strings?"

"Where I live, how Clementine is to be schooled, a prenuptial agreement if I marry again and a dozen more clauses in the will."

"Doesn't change the fact that you're a majority shareholder in Bryant Oil now." He shook his head. "One newspaper article called you the runaway heiress."

"Fake news, and I'm sure that sold a lot of newspapers." She shrugged. "Actually, there is very little about me available online. I've stayed out of the spotlight since I left for college."

"Hard to know what to believe," he murmured.

"Yet, you were willing to believe Slats and what you read online over what I have been telling you for the last fifteen weeks." She rubbed her forehead. "What the papers don't say is that I relinquished any claim on the estate. A team of attorneys and the board of directors of Bryant Oil will run her company. Once the official paperwork is signed, then I'm out of the picture."

"You're going to tell me that you drove a broken-down Honda and lived from hand-to-mouth on purpose when you had a bank account you could have tapped into at any time?"

"I want my daughter to grow up with trust and with unconditional love. Not a love based on rules or financial payoffs. I want her to know there is a God out there who loves her unconditionally, as well. The money has never mattered." Hannah took a deep breath. "My grandmother's money has destroyed my life at every turn."

Hannah stood and paced back and forth, trying to contain the emotions that threatened to erupt. Finally, she stopped and stared out the office window at the stables. She had trusted Tripp Walker with her heart and soul and secrets. He'd let her down, like everyone else. Rejected by one man because she didn't have a fortune and by another because she did.

Suddenly, she was angry. Angrier than she'd been in a long time, because anger didn't come easily to Hannah. She was annoyed and irritated on a regular basis. Especially with Tripp. But never truly angry. She always found a way to see around the issue and back off before she reached a boiling point.

But now…now she was mad enough to do something stupid and that meant it was time to back off and walk away. She pulled her purse out of the bottom drawer and turned to face him.

"You've made yourself judge and juror and found me guilty. The truth is that the only thing I've ever been guilty of is believing in happy endings when clearly since birth, my life has been nothing but betrayals."

She stepped toward the door.

"Where are you going now?"

"I quit."

"We leave for Fort Worth on Thursday. You can't quit until then. We have an agreement." Though he said the words, the fight seemed to have gone out of Tripp.

"Our agreement was broken when you chose to believe Slats over me." She opened the door. "I'll be in Fort Worth for Jane. Because she deserves it. Then I'm leaving."

"That's your specialty, isn't it, Hannah? Leaving?" he murmured.

Her steps slowed at his words. "Maybe so, and maybe someday I'll regret this, but I don't think so."

Hannah kept walking until she was out of the stables and into the sunshine.

"Well, now you've gone and done it," she heard Dutch grumble as she left.

She walked past Jane's pen, her gaze lingering on the copper horse. The mare nickered as if calling out.

"I can't, Jane. I can't. I have to keep moving or I'll never make it to the bunkhouse without breaking down."

Hannah clenched her jaw, fighting off the ache deep in her soul. Jane accepted her unconditionally, and in return, she loved that horse with her whole heart. Now she had to leave her. As if her heart wasn't broken into enough pieces already. Head down, Hannah sniffed and kept walking.

Rue was in the doorway of the bunkhouse with a box in her arms when Hannah arrived.

"Oh, hi there, Hannah. I'm just dragging more of my stuff back to my apartment." She hitched the box higher in her arms. "What are you doing home so early?"

"I…" Hannah stumbled over a response.

Rue peered closer. "Oh, Hannah, is everything all right?"

"No," Hannah said. "Everything is perfectly awful."

"Is there anything I can do?"

"I don't think there's anything anyone can do, Rue." She put her hand on the older woman's arm. "Some days I just have to wonder how I could have so thoroughly and completely missed God. It's like I had my eyes closed when He put up the road signs."

"We all experience that, dear. Trust me." She smiled sadly. "This too shall pass."

"That's normally what I would have said." Hannah released a sad sigh. "But I don't think there's anything about this that's going to pass anytime soon."

"You planning to be like this the whole ride to Fort Worth? If so, it's gonna be the longest five hours of my life," Dutch said.

"Like what?" Tripp scowled and gripped the steering wheel all the harder as he focused on the road and the precious cargo in the horse trailer.

"Like you're waiting to slug someone, that's what." Dutch jammed his hat on his head and crossed his arms. "I tell you, I've had fun before, and this ain't it."

"Why is it you're riding with me, anyhow?" Tripp asked.

"Because Hannah is acting even ornerier than you are and she flat refused to ride with you. Lucy ordered me to. Since she signs my checks, here I sit."

"Great. Just absolutely perfect," Tripp growled.

When Dutch reached out to turn on the radio, Tripp's arm shot out to stop him.

"I'm not listening to that *cry in your beer, miss my horse, my girlfriend doesn't love me* music," he said, instantly irritated.

"We can listen to something else," Dutch said.

"Quiet is good," Tripp returned.

"No, quiet just gives you more time inside your head and I'm not too sure that's a good place for anyone right now."

There was silence for the next few miles before Tripp finally shot a glance at Dutch. "The breadcrumbs were all there," he said.

"Huh? The what?"

"Hannah. I chose to see what I wanted to see." He shook his head. Like Hannah and the letters from Jake Maxwell to her mother. Hannah saw what she needed to see because she desperately needed a family.

He'd seen Hannah as a scheming, irresponsible single mother because that's what he needed to see to once again justify his rotten childhood. Of course, he chose to ignore all the little things along the way that said she wasn't at all what he'd labeled her.

"Aww, get over yerself, will you?" Dutch remarked.

Tripp jerked back at the words. "Excuse me?"

"You're mad at Hannah because it turns out she's not a grifter. Is that about right?"

"No," he started. "No. I didn't say that."

"Sure you did." Dutch snorted. "I didn't notice you speaking up when everyone thought you and she were an item."

"I did that for Clementine."

"Yeah, right. I'm pretty sure you were okay with things when you thought you were the one saving her. When you got to be the hero."

"What's that supposed to mean?"

"Just what I said. You're copacetic if you're the one wearing the cape. Looks to me like you're plum scared because the tables are turned."

"Now you're just insulting me for no good reason."

Dutch kept talking without pause.

"I think you got a whiff of that, which is what's eating you up. Ever think that maybe Hannah and Clementine are saving you?"

Tripp gripped the steering wheel, debating whether he should let the old cowboy walk the rest of the way to Fort Worth. The idea held merit, but Lucy would kill him.

"You listening to me?"

"I don't have much choice, do I?" Tripp asked.

Dutch kept talking. "I think your problem is now you think Hannah is too good for you because of her money."

Tripp glanced over at the old wrangler. "How did you know about the money?"

"Same as you. I tracked down Slats and he told me everything for a small nominal fee."

"You paid him?"

"Sure I did. I'm emotionally invested in Hannah and Clementine. Unlike you, I care about what's going to happen to them even if that slimy cowboy charged me half my paycheck."

He paused. "Rue made you do it, didn't she?"

"That, too. Doesn't matter, I was willing. More than willing."

"By the way, I do care," Tripp added.

"Then act like it. This ain't all about you and your feelings."

Tripp swallowed the ugly truth that Dutch Stevens, of all people, was right.

What could he possibly offer someone like Hannah? She had so much potential, and now that she was no longer hiding, the whole world was hers to grab. She might decide she wanted to be an heiress after all.

Why would she need him in her life?

He was protecting himself from what couldn't possibly end well.

Tripp inhaled and exhaled slowly.

Besides, they had nothing in common, he told himself. Nothing to build a future on. Nothing.

"It's your differences that make a relationship interesting. Not your similarities," Dutch said. "Not much fun to fall in love with a clone of yourself." The old cowboy shot him a look that said that was a particularly unpleasant thought.

Tripp stared at him. Was the crotchety wrangler reading his mind? And who said anything about love?

"What are you looking at?" Dutch asked. "You don't get to be my age without learning a thing or two." He shrugged. "Why do you think Rue and I get along so well?"

Tripp wasn't going to touch that one. He stared out the window for minutes before responding.

"You don't understand, Dutch. That woman is way out of my league. The pitiful part is that I've spent the last three months thinking she was a gold digger. Fighting my feelings and being judgmental because I thought she had a shady history. What a joke. Even worse, what does that say about my judgment?"

"A tad off the mark, I'll give you that. But then you've always been somewhat skewed and cynical in your outlook when it comes to grown-up type people."

"Skewed and cynical? That's not true."

"Sure, it is. You give kids and horses a second chance. You'll go out on a limb to trust them and offer unconditional love. Anyone else? They cross you once and you write them off."

Dutch shook his head. "And cynical?" He laughed. "You wouldn't see a silver lining if it wrapped itself around your big head and tugged."

Tripp turned and glared.

"I'm just saying."

"Don't hold back. Tell me what you really think."

"What I think is that all you young bucks are the same. You get run over by love and you struggle to stand, looking around, trying to figure out what hit you without a clue that what you need to do is grovel and get it over with."

"I'm not in love with Hannah," Tripp roared.

"Whatever you say." Dutch chuckled, unperturbed by the fact that Tripp was now fuming.

"Look, we have a long ride ahead of us and I don't want to spend it talking about Hannah," Tripp said.

"Fine by me. But you and me both know you're gonna be thinking about her all the way down I-35 South."

Tripp took a deep breath and shook his head, knowing the old wrangler was right and hating it.

Chapter Twelve

"What's wrong with Jane?" Dutch asked as he dragged a bale of hay into the stall.

Tripp stepped into the stall and did a quick assessment, running a gentle hand over her flank and abdomen and then inspecting her legs. "Doesn't seem to be a physical ailment, but something is definitely off," Tripp said. "I'm just not sure what."

"What do you mean, you're not sure?" Dutch prodded. "You're the horse whisperer."

"Be that as it may, I don't know what's wrong. Jane flat refuses to budge." He stepped out of the stall. "She was fine at Big Heart Ranch and she's not fine now. That's all I know for sure."

"Did she hurt herself in the trailer?"

"That doesn't appear to be the case."

"That mare has got her face in the corner. That's not good," Dutch said with a frown.

"Thanks for the valuable input, there, pal." Tripp's gaze moved to the center aisle. He glanced around the backstage area of the Fort Worth arena, which was lined on both sides with stalls. The place was huge, with over two thousand horse stalls total in the multiple arenas.

The facility was used for public events in the auditoriums and had an impressive livestock complex and multiple arenas. Underground tunnels connected the equestrian facilities.

Today, the place was busy with cowboys, staff and even the media. There was a buzz of excitement in the air. This was it. The finals. The culmination of everything he'd work for. Could he deliver?

The judges were at the other end of the center aisle right now, but it wouldn't be long before they were right in his face.

"Maybe it's because she's used to being turned out 24/7," Dutch mused. "Or maybe she's just plum mad at you."

"Why would she be mad at me?"

"I can think of a dozen reasons," Dutch muttered.

"She's not mad at me, but I've got to do something before those judges come around with their little clipboards. I could lose forty points before this even begins, and then I'm out of it. One small misstep and we may as well go home. One hundred days of training circling the drain."

The horse had been eating, drinking and eliminating without a problem. Tripp glanced at Jane again, suddenly realizing that Dutch might not be too off the mark.

No, Jane wasn't mad at him. She missed Hannah. Leaving Big Heart Ranch and coming to this strange environment had only intensified the mare's feelings of loss.

Tripp swallowed hard because he knew his next decision meant laying down his pride and doing what was best for the horse. Truth be told, he still wasn't sure eating his hat would save them today, but he had to try.

"What are we going to do?" Dutch asked as he spread the hay around the stall.

"I need Hannah," Tripp admitted. "Right away."

"Hannah ain't even here yet and even if I do find her she's so mad at you I'd be spitting in the wind asking her to help you out. She might be so inclined to give me a piece of her mind, and I guarantee she's real good at that."

Tripp did a double take. "Wait a minute. Why isn't Hannah here yet? I saw her packing up the truck at Big Heart Ranch with Travis and Lucy as we pulled out. They should have been minutes behind us."

Dutch stepped out of the stall and dusted himself off. "They had a flat tire outside of Ardmore. Put them behind schedule."

"Call and make sure they're okay? Would you?"

"I already talked to them an hour ago."

"Dutch, for once can you not argue with me and just call and make sure Hannah is okay?"

"For a man who dismissed the woman a few days ago, you're sure riled up," Dutch scoffed. "Maybe you oughta just quit taking the long way around the barn and apologize to her."

Tripp narrowed his gaze and pulled out his own phone. "Never mind. I'll call Travis myself."

"Hold on. No need." Dutch nodded straight ahead. "Look there. Coming toward us."

Tripp glanced down the long hall, finally spotting Travis and Lucy weaving in and out of the crowd. They were all smiles as they approached. Hannah lagged behind, her gaze on anything but him. He knew he deserved that. He'd been a pigheaded fool, blind to anything but his own feelings.

"Well, would you look at that? Seems to me she don't

look much like an heiress today, does she?" Dutch asked quietly. "She just looks like Hannah."

Tripp shook his head. Okay, fine. Dutch was right. She did just look like Hannah and he was glad to see her. The dark hair floated around her shoulders in waves and she wore a loose maternity blouse with jeans and cowboy boots. Hannah was so trim, you'd have to look twice to notice she was actually pregnant.

But he knew it, and he had a picture of baby Anne sitting on his desk in the bunkhouse.

"Hey, Tripp," Lucy said. "This is so exciting."

"Thanks for coming," Tripp said.

"Are you kidding?" Travis said. "Wouldn't miss this. I'm so excited you're finally going after your dreams."

Was he? Tripp considered the words for a minute. His dreams. This competition was about Jane and Hannah. Yeah, he'd win this for them.

"Thanks, Travis." He turned to Hannah. "May I talk to you? It's about Jane."

"Jane?" Concern filled Hannah's eyes. She looked to Travis and Lucy.

"We'll go find our seats," Travis said. "Come on, Luce."

"What's going on?" Hannah said.

"I need help with Jane. Do you suppose that you and I can put aside our differences for that mare?"

"What's wrong with her?"

Tripp's gaze followed Hannah's as she glanced behind him, searching the stalls for the mare. He could see Jane, and the animal's ears twitched as though she was listening.

"I can't get her to budge from that stall. She misses you. I've got about five minutes until I'm out of the competition before it even begins."

"I didn't mean to upset her. I couldn't bear the thought of her being auctioned off, so I've stayed away the last few days. Kept Clementine away, as well."

Tripp raised a palm. "I get that. No judging here. I just need your help." He glanced down the center of the stable area. "Those fellas with the clipboards are getting closer."

Hannah hesitated, her gaze going from Tripp to the stall.

"Please," he said. "For Jane."

She crossed her arms. "As I recall, you said that you don't want me near her."

"Hannah, I may have been a bit overprotective."

"You think?"

She wasn't going to make this easy, and he was running out of time.

"I was wrong," he said.

"Yes, you were."

Tripp shot a nervous glance down the walkway. "If you could go and talk to Jane… Just go to her stall and talk to her. That mare will do anything for you. I think we both know that."

A determined expression crossed Hannah's face, and she stood straight and proud, meeting his gaze. "Okay, but we do this my way this time, Tripp. I mean it. My way."

"Whatever you say." Tripp nodded and stepped aside as Hannah walked to Jane's stall.

"Jane," Hannah called. "Hey, there, sweet girl."

The mare shook her head, snuffled and offered a low snort as if to say she heard but she wasn't going to forgive that easily.

"I'm sorry, Jane. Please turn around," Hannah cooed. Jane shook her head, then finally nickered and moved, as if considering Hannah's words. A moment later, she slowly stepped in a semicircle until she faced center aisle. Her head dipped over the stall gate to inspect Hannah.

"Aw, she sure loves you, Hannah," Dutch said.

"Grab that stool," Tripp said to Dutch.

"Got it, boss."

Tripp placed the stool outside the stall and helped Hannah to step up. She put her arms around the mare's neck and buried her nose in Jane's mane. The horse held very still as Hannah smoothed her mane and ran a hand over her withers.

He wanted to tell her to be careful, but he kept his mouth shut. Her way, she said.

"Oh, sweet girl, how I've missed you." Then she carefully stepped off the stool and opened the gate. "Come on now, Jane, let's get going."

She handed the lead rope to Tripp and moved aside as Jane walked out of the stall.

The rush of relief slammed into Tripp. "Thank you," he murmured.

"I didn't do it for you. I did it for Jane. This is her time to shine. She's worked hard for this, and she deserves a good home and a family that will love her. If winning this competition will do that, then I'll do whatever you need."

Tripp swallowed the lump in his throat. He'd given Hannah nothing but trouble from the day they'd met, yet here she was, helping him out when his back was against the wall.

Hannah met his gaze. "I'll stay down here until she's tacked up. Just to be sure and send a few pictures to Clementine and Rue." She looked at him. "Are you ready to go into that arena?"

"I've done everything I know to do with that horse up to this point. I'm as ready as I'll ever be."

Hannah put her hand on his arm. "You got this, Tripp. I believe in you."

Tripp stood there for a moment, stunned by the generosity of the woman in front of him and wishing things could be different between them.

"Thank you, Hannah."

She nodded and turned away.

"Only a fool would let her go," Dutch muttered. "Go on and win that competition and then get your saddle back home and fix this mess."

Tripp opened his mouth and then closed it again. There was nothing to say. Dutch was right. Again.

First Jane. And then he'd have the daunting task of making things right with Hannah. He'd stepped in a lot of cow patties lately, and cleaning things up would take some time.

Day one hundred.

Hannah stood in the aisle of the arena, looking over the crowd in the grandstands. They'd really made it to day one hundred of the challenge. Who would have thought that her journey from Missouri would take her to this moment?

She was honored to be in this historic arena. Despite what had happened between her and Tripp, she was glad to see this through and be able to close the door on this chapter of her life. And she was glad she could be here to help Jane.

Above her, the flags of Texas and the United States waved. She scanned the arena, taking in everything, trying to capture every sight, sound and scent from today. Memories to tuck away, because soon enough, she'd be far, far away from this arena and from Big Heart Ranch. All of this would be a memory. A memory of the horse and the man she'd loved and lost.

The day was filled with mixed emotions. There was no doubt in her mind that Tripp would at least take Jane to the final ten. After that, she was going to lose the mare that she had grown to love. This moment was oh so bittersweet.

She'd gone back and forth on attending today, until Lucy pulled a guilt trip on her. The family needed to support Tripp and Emma wasn't feeling well. She had reservations about the Big Heart Ranch equine manager, but at the very least, Jane deserved the support. So Hannah had gotten in the truck to drive here with Travis and Lucy, while Rue kept Clementine for the day.

Now she was glad she'd come. Being here provided one more opportunity to see the beloved mare and would bring Hannah closure. She'd stayed away the last few days, hoping to make their final parting easier. It wasn't easier. Every second that she inched nearer to losing the horse she'd grown to love, her heart ached more.

The air smelled like hay, sawdust, horses and popcorn. Cowboys and cowgirls in tight Levi's, crisply starched Western shirts and cowboy hats stood around chatting, all eyes on the center of the arena, anticipating the action which would soon begin. Hannah walked down the rows of the grandstand to the bright blue seating area where Travis and Lucy waited. Around her, the crowd was settling in, preparing for the event, and the excitement in the arena was undeniably contagious.

"How'd it go?" Travis asked. He stood so she could sit on the other side of Lucy.

"Jane will be fine."

Music blared from the overhead speakers and the crowd got to their feet when a mounted rider carrying the US flag entered the arena and stopped in the center for the singing of the national anthem.

When they sat down, Hannah pointed to the white arena gate. "Look. I see them at the gate. They're going to be up first."

Overhead, the announcer confirmed Hannah's words. "Ladies and gentlemen, competitor number twenty-one, Tripp Walker from Big Heart Ranch in Timber, Oklahoma, riding Calamity Jane."

The gate opened and out rode Tripp and Jane. Completely in synch, they trotted around the entire arena before they began the required maneuvers. The audience was still as if sensing that they were witness to something special.

"They're looking really good," Travis said. "Jane is making smooth transitions, maneuvering like she's been doing this her whole life. Far as I can tell, they haven't missed a thing on technical."

"Very nice work," the announcer added, as though he could hear Travis's words. Cheers and applause said the fans in the stands agreed. "This could be as close to perfect tens as we're going to see today. What a way to start the afternoon, folks."

"They received high numbers. It's all going to depend on the rest of the rides," Hannah said.

"How many horses are competing?" Lucy asked after they'd watched a number of horses and trainers.

"One hundred, and the competition has been spread over two days," Hannah said. "Tripp and Jane are in the last batch. We should find out the standings soon. But as of the last rider they were in the top ten."

"Here are the top ten finalists for our final round."

The moment the announcer said the words the arena fell silent.

When Tripp's name was called, Travis launched from his seat, pumping his fist and hollering, "Woo-hoo!"

"I knew they'd make it," Hannah yelled. "I knew it." She was unable to contain a wide grin of pure joy. Tripp Walker might be relationship challenged, but he lacked nothing in the equine department. The man deserved a win today. So did that horse.

"What's next?" Lucy asked. "This is so exciting."

"Four minutes to set up and four minutes to perform. They'll do the required maneuvers and then the free-style performance," Travis said.

"Gosh, I can barely sit here," Lucy said. "My knees are knocking."

Hannah released the breath she was holding and nodded. She was on the edge of her seat herself as one by one, the ten trainers completed their program. Each performance seemed more amazing than the next, making it more unbelievable that the horses were actually wild one hundred days ago.

When Tripp and Jane came out into the arena, they stopped in the center. Tripp's gaze scanned the crowd until it met hers. He tipped his hat, then patted Jane on the neck and whispered something to her.

Hannah's heart fluttered at the gesture.

"Why, he did that just for you," Lucy murmured. "That was so sweet, Hannah. He's acknowledging you."

A warmth crept up Hannah's neck at Lucy's words.

As promised, Tripp and Jane did a bareback routine that left the audience in the grandstands on their feet begging for more. Clearly, the team was a crowd favorite, and the applause was deafening.

The performances continued until all ten trainers

lined up with their horses in the middle of the arena as
the winners were called.

"First place goes to Tripp Walker and Calamity
Jane."

The arena exploded with noise. Hannah jumped to
her feet, screaming as loud as anyone in the stands.
Lucy grabbed Hannah and hugged her, while Travis
continued to whistle, hoot and holler.

When the horse and rider did a victory ride around
the arena, galloping the perimeter, Hannah stood with
the crowd.

Tripp waved at the cheering arena. Then he dis-
mounted and wrapped his arms around Jane's neck in
a tender showing. He turned and once again searched
the stands for Hannah, and when their gazes met, he
offered a thumbs-up.

Yes, they'd done it. Tamed a wild horse in one hundred days. Hannah put a hand to her chest where her
heart trotted out of control.

Who would have thought? It was only May that she'd
challenged Tripp and they'd begun verbally sparring
until he'd finally agreed.

Hannah closed her eyes for a moment, savoring today's memories. He won. She was so proud of him.

Cameras flashed at the presentation of the check
and all attention in the arena remained focused on the
winners.

"Isn't the auction next?" Lucy asked.

Hannah nodded. She swallowed hard. Jane was going
to be auctioned off. The mare with the velvet eyes. Her
special girl would be gone.

Travis met Hannah's gaze, concern in his eyes. "We
don't have to stay for that. Let's head back to Timber.
We'll stop and congratulate Tripp first, then maybe find

a Sonic drive-through and celebrate with cherry lime-ades."

"I like how you think, Trav," Lucy said. She squeezed Hannah's hand.

"Thanks, Travis," Hannah said. "Why don't I meet you two at the truck? I want to call and check on Clementine."

"Sure," Travis said.

She'd call Clementine and Rue and give them the good news, because she couldn't bear to see Jane again and know that the mare wasn't going back to Big Heart Ranch.

Her heart ached. She'd lost it all.

The man, the horse and the family.

Chapter Thirteen

"But Momma, I don't want to leave." Clementine choked the words out on a heartfelt sob.

"Clementine, it's going to be all right, sweetie." Hannah dropped to the mattress next to the five-year-old, her heart aching along with her daughter's.

"No. It's not all right. I don't want to go. Big Heart Ranch is my forever home, Momma."

"Oh, Clemmie. I wish…" Hannah didn't know what she wished and anything she said would only make her daughter break out in a fresh round of tears. Her little face was bright red with the effort and the orange curls had given up and formed a frizzy halo around her head.

The problem was Hannah wasn't sure everything was going to be all right. She wasn't sure of anything anymore and she was fresh out of plans.

Her daughter remained inconsolable. Her wet and noisy sobs gave way to soft hiccups as Hannah rubbed her back. Finally, after several minutes, Clementine fell asleep.

Hannah took a deep breath. She longed to fall apart but simply didn't have the luxury of a meltdown. So she'd stay strong for her daughter.

"Everything okay?" Rue asked as she knocked gently on the screen door. "I heard her crying."

Hannah eased up from the bed, went to the kitchen and unlocked the door. "She's asleep now. I'm sure she was overtired. I let her stay up late last night when I got back from Fort Worth and then we got up early for church."

"Poor baby," Rue said as she stepped into the kitchen. "What got her started?"

"I pulled out the suitcases."

"Oh." For the first time, Rue seemed without a quick response.

"I should have known better."

"Clementine doesn't want to leave." Rue stated the obvious.

"Would you like a cup of tea?" Hannah asked. "I sure could use one."

"Yes, please." Rue sat down at the table. "Although you understand, I'm about to dive right into your business."

Hannah smiled as she turned the burner on under the kettle and grabbed two mugs from the cupboard. She was going to miss Rue Butterfield. "Thanks for the warning."

"I don't understand how you can think about leaving. You won the competition."

"Tripp won."

"He never would have done that without you, dear. He never could have done it without you."

"It doesn't change things, Rue." The kettle began to whistle, and Hannah poured water into both mugs before sliding the tea box across the table.

"Hannah, Big Heart Ranch is your family. You don't leave family."

"The DNA test said otherwise. I am not family. I don't know what I am."

Rue clucked her tongue. "Don't let anyone hear you say that. Big Heart Ranch is all about family and DNA has nothing to do with the families that fill this place with love."

"You're right, I'm sorry. It's just that it's too awkward to be around…" She glanced over at her daughter to be sure she was asleep. "You-know-who, when he believes that I misrepresented myself."

"Honey, don't you get it? You-know-who loves you. He feels like the ground shifted beneath him and he doesn't know the rules anymore. That's why he lashed out."

"I can't fix this, Rue." Hannah dipped her tea bag into the water. "The next move is his, and until he works things out in his head, there's nothing I can do."

"He's a man, so, unfortunately, that may take a little longer. They tend to be as confused as a cow in a parking lot when it comes to women."

"I don't have the kind of time required for him to figure things out," Hannah said. "I'm not even sure I want him to figure things out."

"Oh, the way I see it, you have all the time in the world." She sipped her tea. "Why, this is about the prettiest season in Oklahoma. Although Emma would argue it was Christmas." She glanced outside where the redbud had begun to change to color, their royal reddish-purple leaves shimmering in the breeze.

"I've lived many places. They're all pretty."

"Not as pretty as Big Heart Ranch." Rue smiled her trademark serene smile. "There is no place on God's earth like Big Heart Ranch, dear."

Hannah didn't know what to say to that because deep in her heart she suspected that Rue was right.

"You know, Clementine is counting on enrolling in kindergarten at the Christian school in Timber, just like her hero, Dub."

"Yes. I'm aware." Another hurdle they'd have to overcome. Convincing Clementine there were other heroes in the world.

"Look, how about if Clementine spends the night with me? She and I will go check on the chickens, and then we'll eat cupcakes, watch some very G-rated movies and paint our nails. A girls' night."

Hannah leaned closer. "You're going to bake?"

"I said eat cupcakes. I bought packaged ones."

"I don't know, Rue, Clementine spent yesterday with you."

"So what? Don't even think about denying me time with my honorary grandchild. Especially when you're telling me you're going to leave." She shot Hannah a stern look. "Besides, you need some alone time to think and maybe she needs a break, too. This is a lot for a five-year-old to try to process."

"Rue."

"Don't *Rue* me. I'll let her get a nap in and then I'll be back around dinnertime to borrow her for the night."

"Thank you."

"No thank-you needed. Now tell me about the finals in Fort Worth."

"Oh, Tripp and Jane were amazing. Never in a million years would anyone guess that Jane had been a wild horse one hundred days ago."

"Calamity Jane won." Rue released a sigh. "Imagine that."

"You should have seen them in the arena. Tripp rode

bareback in the finals freestyle round." Hannah pulled out her phone and scrolled through the pictures.

"Look at that!" Rue exclaimed. "Amazing."

Hannah nodded.

"Success with wild mustangs is based on the relationship and Tripp understands that. Relationships are based on trust, consistency and respect. Always those three."

"Yes, and that's the same with human relationships, isn't it?" Hannah asked.

"But our Tripp hasn't had much experience with relationships. Personal ones. Like a man and a woman."

"Surely he's dated before. I mean he's how old?"

"Thirty-four, I believe. Maybe he has. But not much. In the eight years here on the ranch, he's never dated."

"What? I don't understand. Why not?"

"I suspect it has something to do with his past and I also believe our Tripp sees his scar as a disfigurement." Rue offered a wry smile. "Of course, I'm a family practitioner, not a psychiatrist. So what do I know?"

"Not dating. That doesn't make any sense. He's a very handsome man, and he has so much to offer a woman." Hannah blinked. "Why, he cooks, too."

"I didn't say it made any sense. I'm simply telling you how I see the situation."

Hannah sipped her tea and then met her friend's gaze. "And why is it you're telling me this?"

"Because I'm hoping you'll find it in your heart to give him a second chance."

"Oh, Rue, that was low."

"I'm willing to stoop low if you'll rethink this leaving idea." She put her hand on Hannah's. "You and Clementine are far too dear to me to let you go without a bit of a fight. Especially when I can clearly see your happiness is close enough to pluck from the tree."

"If only it was that easy."

"It is that easy. Pray about it, would you?"

Hannah walked Rue out when she left and then sank into the rocker with her tea in hand. The trees rustled with the wind and for a moment, Hannah imagined she heard Jane. A slow tear slipped from her eye and she quickly wiped it away with the back of her hand. Tears were a waste of time. She'd learned that a long time ago. She'd trust in God and put one foot in front of the other.

Casting all your care upon him; for he careth for you.

"What have I learned from all this?" Tripp leaned on the rake and caught his breath. "Don't want things you can't have." He wiped the sweat from his face with his shirtsleeve and shook his head.

"Are you talking to yourself?"

Tripp jumped and turned around to face Travis Maxwell. The pretty-faced cowboy had a smile on his face. Why was he so happy?

As far as Tripp could tell, things were exceptionally lousy in the world.

"Did you need something?" he grumbled.

"Yeah, I'm trying to figure out why you're mucking stalls. That's not your job. You're the equine manager," Travis said.

"Mucking stalls is the best way that I know of to get thinking time in."

He glanced behind Travis and noted Lucy and Emma bringing up the rear guard. "What is this?" he asked. "An intervention?"

"It may as well be," Lucy said.

"Hannah is leaving," Emma said. She pushed in front of Travis, crossed her arms over her pregnant abdomen and shot him her steely-eyed glare. "What are you going to do about it?"

The youngest Maxwell clearly had a burr under her saddle today. Tripp looked her up and down.

"How is Hannah leaving? She doesn't even have a car. Does she think she can call an Uber or something?" He nearly laughed aloud. Then he realized they were serious.

"Dutch is taking her to the bus station in Pawhuska tomorrow," Lucy said. "You know I'm completely against interfering in your business, Tripp, but you have to do something. You're the only one who can make Hannah stay."

Tripp stared at Lucy as his mind took off like a galloping horse.

Dutch? Why would he do that? Hannah and Clementine belong on Big Heart Ranch. He made a mental note to fire the old wrangler.

He glanced at his watch and handed the rake to Travis. "Here, you finish." Tripp headed toward the exit. "Oh, and lock up my office when you're done."

"Me?"

"Yeah. I blame you for this."

"What? Why?" Travis called.

"You hired Dutch."

He strode out of the stables and across the yard to the bunkhouse he used in the summer months. It was a good thing he hadn't moved back to his apartment in town yet because he was running out of time.

Fortunately, he had a plan. Trouble was he'd been pondering said plan since he got back from Fort Worth last night and so far he hadn't found the courage to put it into motion.

It was now or never. Time to cowboy-up because you only got one chance at a second chance.

He had this. The horse was in the pen. The cake was on the counter and the check was in his wallet. All he had to do was shower and grovel.

He could do that. Right?

Tripp swallowed the fear edging in and walked faster.

It took him ten minutes to shower and dress, collect everything and head over to Hannah's bunkhouse. He had to slow down some so the cake wouldn't flip over and land in the dirt.

"You got this," he repeated over and over. "Grovel and give it your best shot and the rest, well, it's in the good Lord's hands."

His fingers trembled as he knocked on the door.

"Tripp?" Hannah blinked with confusion when she appeared at the screen. "Is there something—?"

"Yes. I brought your check."

She opened the screen door and held it open. "You brought a cake, as well. Come on in."

"Yeah, I was testing out a new recipe." He thrust the cake, tucked neatly in a plastic carrier, into her hands.

"Thank you." Hannah placed the cake on the table. She still looked confused but confused trumped hostile.

"It doesn't sound like you're still mad at me," he said, then nearly slapped himself. What a stupid thing to say.

"I'm annoyed and irritated. Does that count?"

"I like a challenge," he murmured.

"Excuse me?"

Tripp kept talking, counting on the fact that his feet were too big to get them both in at one time.

"I brought your check. Did I mention that yet?"

"My check? Oh, the check from the 100-Day Challenge. The seventy-thirty deal we shook on. The agreement that I broke." She met his gaze. "That check."

"Jane was trained by the time you quit and you only quit because I was a donkey." He pulled the check from his wallet and handed it to her. "It's yours fair and square."

"Thank you." She looked at him. "Do you mind if I sit down? Things have been a little overwhelming lately and my center of gravity is off, as well."

"You all right?" He quickly pulled out a chair for her.

"Fine." She eased into the chair.

"What about the cake?" he asked.

"Cake?" She started to rise. "You want cake now?"

"Sit down. I know where everything is." He grabbed Hannah's two mismatched china plates from the cupboard and opened the drawer for napkins, forks and a server. "Could you take off the cover for me?"

"Sure. I can do that. This must be a very special cake." She depressed the tabs and lifted the cover. Then she released a small gasp. "Red velvet."

"Yeah." He sliced the cake and slid a piece over to her before cutting a sliver for himself. "Food love language," he said.

"I remember." Hannah bit her lip as a pained expression filled her eyes. "Tripp, I don't know what to say."

"There's nothing for you to say. I need to do the talking."

Hannah nodded, and he wasn't sure if she was going to cry or throw something at him.

"I was wrong, Hannah. Completely. I've been overprotective because every time I saw you around a horse I saw my past and how I couldn't save my brother or my mother."

"Oh, Tripp."

He held up a hand. "No. I'm not here for your sympathy, empathy or pity. I'm here to apologize. Let me do that before my brain figures out what I'm doing and I run the other direction."

She nodded.

"Hannah, you were right, I did judge you. I apologize for that, too. I was falling in love with you from day one. The more you made me feel, the more I backpedaled. After all, who was I to love you?"

He met her gaze, finding comfort in the warm brown eyes. "Once I found out you were an heiress, well, that blew everything out of the water."

She sighed. "It's more than a little disturbing that you think I am that shallow and that you think so little of yourself."

He looked away for a moment. It took every bit of courage inside him to meet her gaze once again and allow her to see him raw and vulnerable. "I'm afraid, Hannah. I haven't been this afraid since I was sixteen and walked away from home."

"What are you saying?" Hannah asked. Her expression said that she needed to hear it all. That this was not the time to be economical with his words.

"I'm saying that I should have come to you to ask about your past." He swallowed. "I don't want to have a whatever-maybe relationship with you. I love you and I love Clementine."

She ran a hand through her dark tresses, tangling them into an adorable mess as she most likely battled the same fears he had. "You don't know what you're getting yourself into. I have so much baggage."

"We both have a lot of baggage. I thought maybe we could use our winnings to find a little starter ranch that would have room for you and me and Clementine and the baby and all the baggage."

Hannah laughed.

He reached out and touched her hand. When she didn't pull away, he was buoyed with hope and continued. "I went after the 100-Day Challenge thanks to you. You made me dream a dream that I hadn't even considered chasing. I thought dreams were for other people."

"Tripp, there was never any doubt that you'd win."

"Hannah, I'm nothing but doubts." He stood and tugged her hand. "Come on. I want to show you something."

"Where are we going?"

"Outside." He led her across the yard and the gravel toward the old barn. The scent of hay being baled in the north pasture filled the air.

"What was that?" Hannah turned her head to listen.

As they rounded the corner, the circular pen came into view. Calamity Jane walked toward them, nickering in welcome.

"Jane," Hannah breathed, her voice laced with wonder. "I'd run to that fence, but I'm afraid my running days are over for a few months."

Tripp took her elbow and walked with her to the fence where the mare welcomed her.

"Jane, my sweet girl, it's really you."

"Go ahead, you can climb up on that rail. I'll hold you. Jane wants some loving."

"Thank you, Tripp." She climbed to the first rung, and Tripp's hands held her steady as she hugged Jane. For moments, she murmured endearments to the mare. When she got back on the ground her eyes were moist with unshed tears.

Hannah turned to face him. "Jane says I should marry you."

"Aw, you don't have to marry me because I brought Jane home."

"Tripp Walker, look at me."

"Yes, ma'am." He obeyed and prayed she couldn't tell he was scared to death.

"I love you," Hannah murmured. She lifted her hand and caressed his scar. "I'd love you even if you hadn't brought Jane back to Big Heart Ranch. Now, I just love you more."

Tripp bent his head and whispered, "I love you, too" against her lips, before he wrapped her in his arms for a long, lingering kiss.

Behind them, Jane nudged Tripp's shoulder and nickered in complete agreement.

Epilogue

A year made all the difference in the world. A year ago she arrived at Big Heart Ranch.

Jane nickered and Hannah looked up to see Dutch lead Clementine around the circular pen on the mare's back. Now six years old, almost seven, Clementine wore a pink riding helmet and pink cowboy boots, both birthday gifts from her new daddy, Tripp.

Nestled in Hannah's arms, baby Anne scrunched up her little face and stirred.

Overhead, a robin's egg blue sky was dotted with fluffy cotton clouds. Hannah inhaled when the warm spring breeze stirred the air, bringing with it the scent of Oklahoma red clay, grass and the fragrance of dozens of lilac trees that had been planted years ago on Big Heart Ranch.

Could life get any better than this?

She turned at the sound of boots crunching on gravel. *Tripp.*

Her husband was back from Tulsa, and she offered him a welcoming smile.

Tripp closed the distance between them, wrapping

his arm around her shoulder and pulling her close, his lips warm upon hers.

"I missed my girls," he murmured.

"We missed you, too," Hannah breathed.

"Daddy Tripp!" Clementine called out. "Look, I'm riding almost by myself."

"You'll be ready for the rodeo by summer," he said.

Clementine beamed beneath his praise. "Did you bring me something?" she asked.

"Well, of course. I found those pink hair clips you wanted."

"Oh, thank you."

"Did you bring me something?" Dutch called.

"You bet. Twelve bags of feed. They're still in the truck."

"You're just too generous, boss," the wrangler grumbled as he helped Clementine down from the mare.

Tripp met his wife's gaze and reached into his back pocket. "I brought you something, too."

"What's that?"

He pulled a neatly folded paper out of his back pocket and handed it to her.

Hannah's hand shook as she unfolded the paper.

"They agreed to our offer," Tripp said. "I got the call on my way home and stopped at the real estate office in Timber."

"The ranch and the house?"

"Yeah. They're expediting closing, so the Walker family can be in our new home in two weeks."

Hannah's breath caught, and she leaned against Tripp. "Our own place," she said.

"So what do you think about heading down to Pauls Valley to get a horse for this year's 100-Day Challenge?"

Her eyes widened.

"Fact is, there's no reason why we can't get two horses this year, right? One for each of us."

She nearly gasped at the words. "Really? That's a wonderful idea. I mean, as long as you don't mind if I beat you in the competition."

Tripp released a laugh, his blue eyes twinkling with amusement. "Dream on, Mrs. Walker."

She met his gaze.

"Oh, it's really happening, Tripp."

"Yeah. And the best part is that our place is right down the road from Big Heart Ranch."

Hannah nodded. Yes. She'd always be part of the ranch that gave her a second chance.

"So what's next?" she asked Tripp.

"I'll get you to sign the paperwork as co-owner of Walker Equine."

"Co-owner. I like that."

He kissed her forehead. "Me, too."

Hannah glanced at her watch. "We better head over to the chow hall. That meeting is in five minutes."

A small cry from baby Anne had their immediate attention.

"Your daughter is awake," Hannah said.

"Do you want me to hold her?" he asked.

"Yes, please. But let me warn you. She's been a real squiggle bug today."

"That's because she misses her daddy."

The five-month-old looked up at her father with adoring eyes. He took the baby from Hannah's arms and cradled her against his chest like he'd been doing it all his life. He'd taken so quickly to fatherhood that Rue had dubbed him the baby whisperer.

"What's this meeting about?" Tripp asked.

"It's time to get ready for another year of events at Big Heart Ranch."

Clementine led the way to the chow hall. Just steps ahead of them, she skipped and sang a little song to herself.

Tripp opened the big glass doors for them and then stepped inside where Lucy, Emma and Travis stood at the front of the room preparing for the meeting.

Emma's husband, Zach, walked back and forth, gently rocking five-month-old Zachary Steven Norman. His twin girls, Elizabeth and Rachel, followed him while chattering nonstop.

Across the room, Jack Harris sat at a table feeding eighteen-month-old Daniel, while triplets Ann, Eva and Dub colored with crayons at the table.

The double doors opened again, and AJ Maxwell walked in with Rue and Dutch. AJ carried little Barbara Ellin in her arms. The baby was now nine months old and, as predicted, with her golden curls and bright blue eyes, looked like she belonged on the cover of a parenting magazine.

"Momma, may I go sit with Dub and his sisters?" Clementine asked.

"Okay, but you have to be very quiet during the meeting."

"Yes, Momma."

Planning for another year at Big Heart Ranch included the staff Thanksgiving dinner, the Holiday Roundup, another summer of trail rides, vacation Bible school and the summer rodeo.

All of this would be part of Hannah's life for many years to come. Her children would grow up taking part in this ranch that healed so many hearts.

It didn't escape Hannah that Jake Maxwell had somehow managed to lead her to this place over thirty years ago by writing letters to her mother.

Hannah sighed and reached for her husband's hand.

"I love you," Tripp mouthed.

"I love you, too," she whispered. Her heart was full as she smiled at the cowboy she loved so very much.

By the grace of God, she had been blessed with a second chance that took her to Timber, Oklahoma, and Big Heart Ranch. Home to the people who would be her forever family.

Hannah had been wrong; love did heal all things.

* * * * *

If you loved this story, pick up the other books in the Big Heart Ranch series from beloved author Tina Radcliffe:

Claiming Her Cowboy
Falling for the Cowgirl
Christmas with the Cowboy

Available now from Love Inspired!

Find more great reads at
www.LoveInspired.com

Dear Reader,

Thank you so much for joining me for this final installment in the Big Heart Ranch series.

Once again, we travel to Timber, Oklahoma, and the Maxwell family ranch for orphaned, abused and neglected children, where unconditional love and the good Lord reign.

Tripp Walker and Hannah Vincent's love story is perhaps one of my favorites as it represents the fears and insecurities we all battle.

Writing this story was not without its challenges as I dug deep into their pasts to uncover the hurts and the dreams of two imperfect people made whole by God's healing love as the Lord of second chances.

I hope you enjoy this tender and romantic story and its wonderful and humorous supporting cast that includes the wise Rue Butterfield and hilariously cantankerous Dutch Stevens.

Do drop me a note and let me know your thoughts. I can be reached through my website, www.tinaradcliffe.com, where you can also find Hannah and Tripp's chili recipes. Additionally, Tripp was finally persuaded to share his secret carrot cake recipe.

Enjoy!

Sincerely,
Tina Radcliffe

COMING NEXT MONTH FROM
Love Inspired®

Available March 19, 2019

THE AMISH SPINSTER'S COURTSHIP
by Emma Miller

When Marshall Byler meets Lovey Stutzman—a newcomer to his Amish community—it's love at first sight. Except Lovey doesn't believe the handsome bachelor is serious about pursuing her. And with his grandmother trying to prevent the match, will they ever find their way to each other?

THEIR CONVENIENT AMISH MARRIAGE
Pinecraft Homecomings • by Cheryl Williford

The last thing widowed single mother Verity Schrock expects is to find her former sweetheart back in town—with a baby. Now the bishop and Leviticus Hilty's father are insisting they marry for their children's sake. Can a marriage of convenience cause love to bloom between the pair again?

THE RANCHER'S LEGACY
Red Dog Ranch • by Jessica Keller

Returning home isn't part of Rhett Jarrett's plan—until he inherits the family ranch from his father. Running it won't be easy with his ranch assistant, Macy Howell, challenging all his decisions. But when he discovers the truth about his past, will he begin to see things her way?

ROCKY MOUNTAIN DADDY
Rocky Mountain Haven • by Lois Richer

In charge of a program for foster youths, ranch foreman Gabe Webber is used to children...but fatherhood is completely different. Especially since he just found out he has a six-year-old son. Now, with help from Olivia DeWitt, who's temporarily working at the foster kids' retreat, Gabe must learn how to be a dad.

HER COLORADO COWBOY
Rocky Mountain Heroes • by Mindy Obenhaus

Socialite Lily Davis agrees to take her children riding...despite her fear of horses. Working with widowed cowboy Noah Stephens to launch his new rodeo school is a step further than she planned to go. But they might just discover a love that conquers both their fears.

INSTANT FATHER
by Donna Gartshore

When his orphaned nephew has trouble at school, Paul Belvedere must turn to the boy's teacher, Charlotte Connelly, for assistance. But as the little boy draws them together, can Paul trust Charlotte with his secret...and his heart?

LOOK FOR THESE AND OTHER LOVE INSPIRED BOOKS WHEREVER BOOKS ARE SOLD, INCLUDING MOST BOOKSTORES, SUPERMARKETS, DISCOUNT STORES AND DRUGSTORES.

LICNM0319

Get 4 FREE REWARDS!

We'll send you 2 FREE Books plus 2 FREE Mystery Gifts.

Love Inspired® books feature contemporary inspirational romances with Christian characters facing the challenges of life and love.

FREE Value Over **$20**

YES! Please send me 2 FREE Love Inspired® Romance novels and my 2 FREE mystery gifts (gifts are worth about $10 retail). After receiving them, if I don't wish to receive any more books, I can return the shipping statement marked "cancel." If I don't cancel, I will receive 6 brand-new novels every month and be billed just $5.24 for the regular-print edition or $5.74 each for the larger-print edition in the U.S., or $5.74 each for the regular-print edition or $6.24 each for the larger-print edition in Canada. That's a savings of at least 13% off the cover price. It's quite a bargain! Shipping and handling is just 50¢ per book in the U.S. and 75¢ per book in Canada.* I understand that accepting the 2 free books and gifts places me under no obligation to buy anything. I can always return a shipment and cancel at any time. The free books and gifts are mine to keep no matter what I decide.

Choose one: ☐ **Love Inspired® Romance Regular-Print** (105/305 IDN GMY4) ☐ **Love Inspired® Romance Larger-Print** (122/322 IDN GMY4)

Name (please print)

Address   Apt. #

City   State/Province   Zip/Postal Code

Mail to the **Reader Service:**
IN U.S.A.: P.O. Box 1341, Buffalo, NY 14240-8531
IN CANADA: P.O. Box 603, Fort Erie, Ontario L2A 5X3

Want to try 2 free books from another series? Call 1-800-873-8635 or visit www.ReaderService.com.

---

*Terms and prices subject to change without notice. Prices do not include sales taxes, which will be charged (if applicable) based on your state or country of residence. Canadian residents will be charged applicable taxes. Offer not valid in Quebec. This offer is limited to one order per household. Books received may not be as shown. Not valid for current subscribers to Love Inspired Romance books. All orders subject to approval. Credit or debit balances in a customer's account(s) may be offset by any other outstanding balance owed by or to the customer. Please allow 4 to 6 weeks for delivery. Offer available while quantities last.

Your Privacy—The Reader Service is committed to protecting your privacy. Our Privacy Policy is available online at www.ReaderService.com or upon request from the Reader Service. We make a portion of our mailing list available to reputable third parties that offer products we believe may interest you. If you prefer that we not exchange your name with third parties, or if you wish to clarify or modify your communication preferences, please visit us at www.ReaderService.com/consumerschoice or write to us at Reader Service Preference Service, P.O. Box 9062, Buffalo, NY 14240-9062. Include your complete name and address.

LI19R

They'd both just turned back to their work when a familiar
loud, croaking sound cut the silence.

The twins shrieked and ran from where they'd been
playing into the little cabin's yard and slammed into Anna,
their faces frightened.

"What was that?" Anna sounded alarmed, too, kneeling
to hold and comfort both girls.

"Nothing to be afraid of," Sean said, trying to hold back
laughter. "It's just egrets. Type of water bird." He located
the source of the sound, then went over to the trio, knelt
beside them, and pointed through the trees and growth.

When the girls saw the stately white birds, they gasped.

"They're so pretty!" Anna said.

"Pretty?" Sean chuckled. "Nobody from around here
would get excited about an egret, nor think it's especially
pretty." But as he watched another one land beside the first,
white wings spread wide as it skidded into the shallow
water, he realized that there was beauty there. He just hadn't
noticed it before.

That was what kids did for you: made you see the world
through their fresh, innocent eyes. A fist of longing clutched
inside his chest.

The twins were tugging at Anna's shirt now, trying to get
her to take them over toward the birds. "You may go look

as long as you can see me," she said, "but take careful steps by the water." She took the bolder twin's face in her hands. "The water's not deep, but I still don't want you to wade in. Do you understand?"

Both little girls nodded vigorously.

They ran off and she watched for a few seconds, then turned back to her work with a barely audible sigh.

"Go take a look with them," he urged her. "It's not every day kids see an egret for the first time."

"You're sure?"

"Go on." He watched her run like a kid over to her girls. And then he couldn't resist walking a few steps closer and watching them, shielded by the trees and brush.

The twins were so excited that they weren't remembering to be quiet. "It caught a *fish*!" the one was crowing, pointing at the bird, which, indeed, held a squirming fish in its mouth.

"That one's neck is like an S!" The quieter twin squatted down, rapt.

Anna eased down onto the sandy beach, obviously unworried about her or the girls getting wet or dirty, laughing and talking to them and sharing their excitement.

The sight of it gave him a melancholy twinge. His own mom had been a nature lover. She'd taken him and his brothers fishing, visited a nature reserve a few times, back in Alabama where they'd lived before coming here.

Oh, if things were different, he'd run with this, see where it led…

Don't miss
Lee Tobin McClain's Low Country Hero,
available March 2019 from HQN Books!

www.Harlequin.com

Looking for inspiration in tales
of hope, faith and heartfelt romance?

Check out **Love Inspired**® and
Love Inspired® **Suspense** books!

New books available every month!

CONNECT WITH US AT:

Facebook.com/groups/HarlequinConnection

Facebook.com/HarlequinBooks

Twitter.com/HarlequinBooks

Instagram.com/HarlequinBooks

Pinterest.com/HarlequinBooks

ReaderService.com